PRIZE FIGHTER

Geonn Cannon

Supposed Crimes LLC • Matthews, North Carolina

This book is a work of fiction. Names, characters, places, and incidents are products of the author's imagination or are used fictitiously. Any resemblance to actual events or locales or persons, living or dead, is entirely coincidental.

All Rights Reserved
Copyright © 2020 Geonn Cannon

Published in the United States.

ISBN: 978-1-952150-02-9

www.supposedcrimes.com

This book is typeset in Goudy Old Styl

Chapter One

"Fire Hill Road was released to mixed reviews. The film holds a 57% rating from Rotten Tomatoes based on 44 reviews. Considered a box office disappointment, the film has gained a cult following due to the rising stars in its cast, including Nathan Sargent, Ida Day, and Renee Lamar in her film debut. (source - Wikipedia)"

There were people who had never been punched in the face. In fact, Maxine Reszke was pretty sure that was the majority of the population. It was a safe bet that she'd taken more knuckles to the cheekbone than anybody in most of the rooms she found herself in. She balanced it out with the knowledge that she'd also probably hit more people in the face than anyone she might meet. The give and take was important.

The other occupants of the room in which she was currently sitting might actually prove a challenge to that belief. Two guys at the pool table had more tattoos than words in their vocabulary, a slick-haired man in a suit who was obviously slumming, and a guy in a denim jacket near the door who was checking a flip phone. She saw them all in the reflection of the TV over the bar which had been out of service for the past two weeks. There was a glass of whiskey in front of her with three full ice cubes and a sliver of alcohol clinging to the bottom.

She didn't like being hit. She didn't necessarily seek it out. But there was something about the point of impact which was unlike any other feeling in the world. Sound cut out. Light crystallized. She could hear blood in her ears, feel the bone under her skin, sense the pull of gravity on her as surely as if there were strings on her shoulders and hips. The evidence of each punch remained on her face, in the line of her nose or the slight puffiness around one eye. The right side of her jaw was uneven, something that could really only be noticed by touch.

Denim Jacket's phone chimed. Max looked over her shoulder. In her periphery, she saw the pool players turn as well. Denim was already moving through the door. Everyone in the bar went back to their own business.

It had been weeks since she was punched hard enough to rattle her cage. There were the occasional fights, but only with students and other beginners who either pulled back at the last second or didn't know how to throw a punch in the first place. It was enough to keep her limber, but it was nothing compared to the real thing. The thrill of a true match, against an opponent who could hold their own against her. That was what she craved more than anything.

Marcus came out of the kitchen with a takeout container in a white plastic bag. She could smell the fries and charred meat as soon as the door swung open. The bar was out of her way, the burger was twice as expensive as what she could get at a fast-food place, and it took him almost a half hour to fill a single order, but it was worth all that hassle for the finished product. She fished her last twenty out of her pocket and dropped it on the bar next to her mostly empty glass.

"No mustard?" she said.

He looked offended she would ask and put the bag down without answering. He scooped up the money and her glass with the same move, turning his back on her as she slipped off the stool with her dinner. The slumming businessman watched her go but she ignored his gaze, and the feeling of it lingering on her when she was past the booth.

The bar was at the end of an alleyway. Fire escape on the right, dumpsters on the left. It was that kind of place, a place no one came willingly or by accident. There was a paper OPEN sign in the window but no other attempt at marketing. Denim was standing near the mouth of the alley facing out, a woman in a black overcoat stood facing him. Her hood was up, and she kept twisting her neck to look toward the street and both ways up the sidewalk. Their heads were bowed toward each other and both stopped talking when Max passed. She'd seen this sort of thing enough times that she barely even registered it.

But then the woman snapped her head toward Max. Their eyes locked. Max held the other woman's gaze for two steps before the woman's nervousness made her look away again.

Max left the alley and turned left. She heard their conversation start up again but only a few words reached her.

"~what you want, that's what~"

"~bring that much. I brought the usual~"

"~come back when you have~"

"~need it now. I promise~"

The woman raised her voice, desperate. The man raised his voice in response. "If you can't afford it, I can find plenty of folks who can."

"I can afford it, but I'm not going to bring that much money to meet a person like you."

"What'd you say, bitch?"

Max was almost to the corner, almost to Not My Problem. But then the woman yelped, followed by a slap. Max stopped. Her burger was going cold with each passing second. She looked back. The sidewalk behind her was empty, but she heard the woman make a high-pitched noise. Like an animal being cornered. Max thought about how long it had been since she'd punched or taken a punch. Even longer if she didn't count the punches she took in the ring.

She sighed. She turned around.

There was just enough distance to get a good running start. She rounded the corner into the alley. Denim had the woman pressed against the wall, one hand over her mouth, the other rifling through the pockets of her coat. Max lowered her head, leading with her shoulder. Neither of them saw Max until she crashed into Denim and sent him flying into the dumpster. The woman shrieked. Denim managed to stay on his feet but stared at Max, dazed.

Max took advantage of his confusion. She grabbed a handful of his jacket and pulled him toward her, brought him close enough to pop him in the face. The blow rocked his head back, but she kept him upright so she could drive her fist forward a second time, then a third, and a fourth. Her knuckles sang, a cool shimmering feeling before the nerves could process the sensation as pain. Denim was breathing through blood now, sputtering, his eyes open but unfocused on anything.

She shoved him hard against the side of the dumpster and put a hand on his forehead to make him look at her.

"Two choices," she said. "You run right now, or I break both your legs so you can't follow her."

He swayed on his feet, and she stepped to one side, shoving him toward the mouth of the alley. He put one hand up to his face as he shambled onto the sidewalk. He veered to one side and bumped his shoulder roughly on the corner of the building, and then slumped out of sight. Max watched him go and noticed her bag of food lying on the sidewalk. She hadn't even noticed dropping it. She walked past the woman she'd saved and bent down to retrieve it. Some gunk on the bottom of the bag, and the burger might have to be reconstructed, but otherwise fine.

"I don't..." The woman sounded on the verge of hysterics. "I-I don't know h-how..."

"Are you good?" Max asked.

The woman blinked. Big eyes. Green or blue, it was hard to tell in the dark. But the hair that had fallen free of her hood was definitely red. It curled along her cheekbone. After a moment she realized what Max was asking.

"Y-yeah. He, he was only looking f-for money."

Max nodded and turned around. She started walking away.

"Wait, I don't know your name..."

"It would be strange if you did," Max said over her shoulder. She raised her hand, using two fingers to sloppily salute the woman as she walked away.

She was almost to her car when she passed Denim sitting on a stoop, hands up over his ruined face. She was pretty sure he was crying. He looked up when he heard her coming and tensed, pressing himself back as if he could melt into the stairs. She held eye contact long enough to cement their dynamic - he was never going to get revenge on her, never try to one-up her if their paths crossed again, because he knew she was choosing to let him go without further injury. She saw the knowledge in his eyes before she put him behind her, literally and figuratively.

Her car was just ahead. She still had time to get home and eat her burger before it turned into cold mush, and she could comfort herself with the knowledge she'd done a good deed.

Stupid.

Renee Lamar's hands were still shaking, and she felt like she was going to throw up. She started walking after her mysterious savior vanished into the night. The stranger had just picked up the dropped bag of food and strolled away like it was nothing. Like the past thirty seconds weren't the most vicious thing she'd ever done. Renee could still hear the sound of the punches. Solid sounds, but sickeningly liquid at the same time, like she was punching a water balloon. And the blood...

She stopped on the corner and realized she would have to get home somehow. She took out her phone, flashing back to Griffin's hands rummaging through them. He was just looking for money, but it could have gone so wrong so easily. And when he found out she didn't have more cash, if that woman hadn't come back, then who knows what might have...

Renee closed her eyes. Took a breath. Let it out. She managed to keep her fingers steady enough to call an Uber. Alvin would be there in two minutes, according to the app. She put the phone back in her pocket and reached up to tuck her hair back under her hood. She stepped under an awning next to the entrance of a closed vape shop to wait for the car.

She took the chance to compose herself. She caught her breath. She made her hands stop shaking and put them in her pocket. Touching the baggie there calmed her somewhat, even though she hadn't yet partaken of it. Just knowing she had it was enough to take the edge off so she could act normally.

A car pulled up to the curb, a lit sign on the rearview mirror announcing it as an Uber. The driver's window rolled down and a man whose beard gave his face an unnaturally round shape.

"Norma?"

Renee smiled. "That's me."

At least it was the name she used on apps like this. She didn't know if it was egotistical to hide her real name, but she didn't want to take any chances. To Uber, Lyft, DoorDash, Amazon, or any company with access to her home address, she was Norma Baker, a nod to Marilyn Monroe's birth name. That was also probably egotistical, but she didn't care. She would rather be slightly safer and full of herself than just listing her name on any app she downloaded.

She got into the backseat. John looked at her in the rearview mirror. "There are chargers back there if you need 'em. Bottle of water, bag of pretzels..."

"I'm fine. Thank you."

He pulled away from the curb and headed north, following the blue line on the phone mounted next to the steering wheel.

Renee sighed and rested her head against the window, staring out at the street. *Stupid*, she thought again. For letting her stash get so low, for not going to her usual guy because he was out of town, for agreeing to meet with someone she'd never actually met in a place he'd chosen. But desperate times. And she was desperate. She knew the area was shady, so she had only taken exactly as much money as she usually needed.

Griffin had recognized her as soon as he walked out of the bar. "Hey, I know you." And that was probably when he decided the price had gone up. The smart thing would've been to walk away, but she'd already seen what was in his hand. She was so close to it, so close to a fix. Just a handful of little white pills, not even a full bottle's worth, and even that cost a couple hundred dollars. There was no chance she was going to bring extra to this part of town.

She closed her eyes and clutched the bag in her pocket like it was a security blanket. She drifted off just enough to be startled when the car pulled to the curb and she opened her eyes to see the house under construction on the corner of her street. She sat up and smoothed her hand over her hair. She wished she had something to tip the driver with. That was one thing she missed about cabs. Handing over the cash was a nice, solid end to the transaction. It was awkward with everything done through the app.

"Well, thank you…"

"No problem." He twisted to look at her. "You know who I was thinking you look like…"

She smiled, already twisting to get out of the car. "Oh, yeah. I get that all the time, believe me."

She closed the door before he had a chance to respond and waited until he pulled away from the curb before she started walking. It was a posh neighborhood in the Pacific Palisades, the sort of place where the risk of walking alone at night was tiny compared to being dropped off at her doorstep. The fresh air also helped calm her nerves and put the events of the night behind her. To her left, the ground dropped away to give the houses along this road an unobstructed view of the ocean, which was currently inky black and reflecting the low-hanging clouds.

She arrived home. The curved stone steps leading up to her door were flanked on either side by solar-powered lights, which made her think of runways and late-night landings. She let herself into the house, silenced the warning beep of her security alarm, and let her coat slide off her arms. When she tapped the sensor on the wall, soft lighting spread out across the open area of her living room. It looked more like a hotel lobby than a home; a square of chairs and divans to her left, and directly ahead, a kitchen where the check-in desk would be.

"Alexa," she said, stepping out of her shoes, "shuffle blues playlist."

Music started playing as she went into the kitchen. The lights were still off here, but she could see well enough in the ambient light to do what needed to be done. She hummed along with the music and ignored the tremors in her fingers as she crushed a few pills and used a knife to push the powder into a blunt line. She bent down, pressed her thumb against one side of her nose, and inhaled deeply.

The oxycodone hit her hard, fast, and complete. She stood up straight, eyes closed as the cool numbness spread through her. Her hands came up and pushed her hair back, thick red handfuls of it, and she rolled her head back on her shoulders. It felt like every part of her - head, arms, legs - was only attacked to her body by thin balloon strings.

After that, her attention drifted in and out but she caught snippets of what she was doing. Slacks and silk panties pooled on the hardwood of the hallway. Her stash was kept in an antique teapot on her bureau with her jewelry. She ran the pad of her middle finger over the design, smiling at how the light glinted off all the rings and necklaces and bracelets surrounding it. She felt like a dragon with her hoard. She chuckled and added the pills to the teapot, then patted the lid when it was back in place.

More flashes rather than actual memories: The snap of the bathroom light coming on. The cold porcelain of the tub under her ass, the splash of water, and then the coldness of it as she sank down. She was still in her bra but otherwise naked. She thought about taking it off, but it was already wet and she didn't feel like making the effort.

She thought about her savior. The mystery woman with her downturned lips, the dark eyes which had locked on Renee's, the extremely short black hair that still managed to make spider-legs over her forehead. Renee saw the roll of the woman's shoulders as she walked, a strut, a challenge to anyone who might be in her way. She wasn't the sort of person to go around. People moved for her.

She was wearing a hoodie. When she walked away she saw a logo on the back. Yellow circle. Palm tree in the center. Words written around the upper arc.

COSTELLO'S BOXING GYM.

"Costello," she murmured.

The blues coming from the living room paused. "When I Was Cruel No. 2" by Elvis Costello began playing. She opened her eyes at the change and wanted to switch it back, but lacked the energy or motivation. Besides, the slow lounge crawl of the song was actually much better than what it replaced, so she dropped her hands into the water and moved her head to the rhythm. She was too far from the speaker to hear the sneering lyrics but that was fine.

An image of the street filled her mind. Her, cowering. The savior, standing in a spotlight. Shoulders rising and falling with her ragged breathing, blood dripping from her fists. She let that memory settle at the forefront of her brain as she drifted away, mouthing the repetitive "Un... un..." from the Costello song.

Max put her left hand flat on her kitchen counter and dropped a bag of frozen broccoli on top of it. The cold seeped into her stinging knuckles, and she ate her dinner with the other hand. Her skin was so hot that she was afraid it might melt the ice. She couldn't catch her breath. The adrenaline wore off when she was halfway home and she broke out into a cold sweat in the car. Even now she felt as if she was burning off every calorie as quickly as she could devour them, taking big animalistic bites of her burger and staring off into the middle distance.

She focused on nothing, because her mind's eye was focused on a memory. "*Reszke was the favorite to win this match, but these first two rounds have been showing none of that promise.*" She hadn't heard their voices at the time, of course, but she'd watched the tape countless times since. Who else had a professional commentary for the worst night of their lives? Who else could supplement their personal point of view with multiple camera angles professionally filmed by HBO?

"*Reszke has landed jab after jab, to seemingly no cumulative effect. You can see the exhaustion in her eyes as she keeps chipping away at this brick wall.*"

"*You definitely can, Jim, but she's a superlative fighter. She's not going to just lay down.*"

She was wearing blue gloves. She sometimes still saw the flashes of blue in her periphery as she threw punches at Miriam Rudd, in her red gloves. Seven rounds. Close to half an hour. Ears ringing, blood pounding in her temples, cuts throbbing and seeping blood down toward her eyes. Her legs shaking from the effort of keeping her upright. She couldn't lose. She *wouldn't* lose.

She heard the bell.

She came out swinging.

Miriam Rudd ducked the swing and landed another hook, Max reeled. She saw the world spin. She remembered feeling like she had a string at the back of her neck that was dangling her just above the ground. But she didn't fall. She faced her opponent and summoned everything she had left. They weren't going to go the full twelve rounds. She knew Rudd was going to win with a KO, but Max wasn't going to go down with anything remaining in the tank.

Max had no memory of the next combination, so she only knew what happened thanks to the videos. Five jabs, a left hook, another left, a right, a jab. Rudd was back on her heels, gloves up near her head as she retreated. Max advanced on her, brow furrowed, eyes dark, a "woman possessed," according to the announcers.

And then a right hook, connection with Rudd's jaw.

Rudd's whole body going rigid, spinning on the balls of her feet, tumbling like a felled tree. Max's memory returned the moment Rudd hit the mat. She remembered seeing, hearing, and feeling the taller British woman hit the mat. The ref rushed in. Rudd's team. Medics. On the video, Max stood above Rudd, lips puffed out by her mouthguard, staring down like a sleepwalker, swaying on her feet as she was announced the winner by knockout.

An hour later, the news revealed Miriam Rudd had slipped into a coma.

Twelve hours after that, she was declared dead.

A once-in-a-lifetime accident. One punch, leading to a subdural hematoma. The death was declared accidental, and Max faced no criminal charges for what happened.

She looked at the bag melting on her hand. It was lumpy and misshapen, half-melted. The burger was long gone, and the fries were no longer crispy. She ate them anyway, even though they tasted like mush in her mouth now. She'd felt that same blind rage when she was attacking Denim Jacket in the alley. She'd felt herself losing control even though she knew how easily it could go wrong.

Max pushed the bag off her hand, flexed her still-red but now chilled fingers. It hurt, but she didn't mind that. She liked hurting.

Her food was gone, so she pushed away from the counter and grabbed her hoodie. She would run to the ocean, taking the long route. It would exhaust her, and it would take at least two hours, so she'd most likely be late to work in the morning. Costello would be pissed, but she didn't care. She had to get rid of this dark energy.

She grabbed her hoodie and pulled it on as she left, flipping the hood up over her head on the way down the stairs. She started running and felt the buzz at the back of her head. She saw Miriam Rudd, she saw Denim Jacket, felt their faces under her fists.

Maybe she would make two laps.

CHAPTER TWO

"...AFTER A smattering of TV roles and a turn among the ensemble cast of Fire Hill Road *earlier this year, Renee Lamar is given the task of carrying the majority of* Lady Strange *on her shoulders. Fortunately she proves herself more than capable of the task, elevating every scene with her mere presence. This is a debut in every sense of the word, and I look forward to what Lamar brings us next."*

Costello's was in Santa Monica, tucked away in a very bleak stretch of nameless businesses. The buildings announced themselves with cheap signs artlessly declaring their services: CAR PARTS, LIQUOR, MASSAGE. The only color came from sickly-thin trees and graffiti that was so beautiful that it might be mistaken for official advertising. It was less than ten miles from Beverly Hills ("Swimming pools, movie stars") but it might as well have been another continent. The Uber driver had even paused when he looked at his screen and saw her destination.

"You sure that's where you want to go? You might be looking for something closer to the beach."

She assured him the address was correct and he gave a head-shake as he pulled away from the curb. Now that she was here, she could understand his reluctance. It wasn't necessarily the bad part of town, but it lacked any kind of glitz or glamour. The boxing gym bucked the neighborhood trend by offering its name on a sign near the door, too small to be seen from the street and lacking information such as hours of operation or what exactly they did.

Renee walked past it three times before she noticed the sign. Even when she saw it, she hesitated before going inside. If it was closed or some kind of membership-only establishment, they might not take very kindly to someone just walking in off the street. But she had come this far, and being kicked out would at least be closure to the journey.

She'd woken up in the tub, water turned icy cold and Alexa still cycling through her Elvis Costello albums, and all she remembered everything about the night before. Griffin, the attack, the last minute save. But the only thing that seemed real was the mystery woman in the grey hoodie with a white bag of takeout dangling from her fingers. She had a craving to find her that was almost as sharply real as the craving that sent her into the alley in the first place. It might have been easier to fight the urge if she didn't have any leads.

But Costello's was just a Google search away, just ten minutes on the Pacific Coast Highway. She couldn't ignore it knowing answers might be so close. She couldn't walk away now that her hand was on the door. So she pushed it open and stepped out of the daylight and into the cold cavern of the gym.

She waited in the doorway a moment for her eyes to adjust. The sounds reached her first: the repetitive padded thump of gloves against heavy bags, sneaker squeaking against concrete, heavy footsteps pounding on canvas stretched tight as a drum. The gym looked more like a garage with workout equipment placed at random angles. There were three boxing rings in the center of the space, only one of which was occupied by two shirtless men in the middle of a sparring session. Two men at the back were facing off against hanging bags. The wall to her left was lined with lockers like the kind she'd had in high school, only significantly more battered.

"Help ya?"

She turned toward the voice. The office in that corner was an obvious afterthought, a square of unpainted drywall with a window that looked out toward the entrance. A man had just come out of it, button-down shirt open over a green long-sleeved shirt that bulged with the bowl of his stomach. She could tell from his chest and shoulders that he'd once been a fighter, and she assumed he was the gym's namesake.

"I hope you can," she said, as genial as she could muster. "I'm looking for someone I believe works here. Or maybe works out here."

He stopped a few feet away from her. "Got a name?"

"Renee."

"Yeah, I know who you are, I meant the person you're looking for."

"Oh." She was embarrassed both at the misunderstanding and that she'd been recognized. "Sorry, um. No, actually I didn't catch a name."

He squinted slightly, a pitying look. "Well, that might make it a touch difficult for me to help you."

"Right." She looked toward the others in the gym. One man at the hanging bags had stopped to look at her, but quickly averted his gaze when she caught him. "Maybe I can describe her. Um, black hair, she's kind of blocky-shaped..."

Costello waved his hand. "Whoa, her? You said her?"

"Yes."

"Why did you think she comes here?"

"She was wearing a hoodie with the logo of this place on the back."

He hooked a thumb over his shoulder, indicating his own back. "Yellow circle, palm tree?" She nodded, and then he nodded as well. "Yeah, that ain't been the logo of this place since my dad was running things. Only a couple of ladies come here, and only one of them still wears that raggedy antique. You're looking for Max."

Renee couldn't believe she had actually tracked down the mystery woman. "Do you know when she might be back?"

"Supposed to be here now," he said. "Shift starts at eleven. Of course the number of times she's ever actually been here at eleven is a lower number than I'd like to admit."

"She works here?"

"Janitor."

Renee was surprised. Given Max's build and fighting ability, the idea of a boxing gym just made sense. She'd assumed the lady was a boxer because she moved and fought like one.

Costello was still talking through her confusion. His lips were too moist and plump and tended to purse when he formed words. It made him look unfortunately like those fish who suction up against aquarium glass. "Go through that door at the back, turn right, and at the top of the stairs."

"I'm sorry? What-what's at the top of the stairs?"

"Maxine, Max. She lives up there. Don't ask me how you can live on top of your workplace and be consistently late to work, but she manages to pull it off. Say whatever you need ta say and then tell her if she doesn't get her butt down here she's goin' ta be unemployed and homeless both."

He turned and went back to the office, leaving Renee to either follow his directions or turn tail and leave. The man at the bags was looking at her again, and now the men in the ring had also noticed her presence. She lowered her head and walked quickly to the back of the gym so she could get outside before anyone recognized her or gained the courage to approach.

She had just reached the door when one of the boxers shouted, "I saw your tits!"

Renee ignored him as she pushed through the back exit and found herself in an alley. She ascended the stairs and found a second story landing littered with worn-out shoes, a pair of boots, and sandals piled in one corner. An empty planter stood next to the door like an ineffectual guard, filled with thick black dirt that almost looked volcanic.

She knocked on the door and stepped back, looking toward the mouth of the alley. There wasn't much of a view; just flat rooftops stretching to the north without even palm trees to remind her she was in California. She was about to knock again when she heard clattering from the other side of the door.

A woman shouted, "Wait a goddamn minute!"

Renee blinked. "Um... I-I'm sorry."

"Shit. Hold on."

Another clattering. The door opened to reveal the woman from the night before. She was still squirming into a sweatshirt, so Renee got a glimpse of her stomach and the boxer shorts she was wearing before the hem fell into place. Max tugged on the bottom and the stretched-out collar fell off one shoulder. She reached up and shook a hand through her hair, though Renee was baffled as to what purpose the move was supposed to serve; it ended up messier than before.

Max blinked and squinted at her, one hand on the door, striking as casual a pose as she could muster while not wearing pants.

"Sorry, who are you?"

"Renee. I'm Renee Lamar. We... w-we sort of... met last night."

The expression of confusion remained on Max's face for a beat. Finally she nodded. "Oh. Right. Sorry." She touched her hair again, looking more confused. "How did you find me?"

"Your hoodie. It had the name of the gym on the back."

Max nodded. She stood there in silence. Finally she tilted her head and narrowed her eyes. "So."

Renee realized she'd spent so much time pushing herself to get here that she hadn't thought about what she was going to do or say when she actually found her savior. She could pay her for what she'd done, but was that tacky? Offensive? She could at least say thank you, but that didn't seem like anything near enough for what she'd done. Max cocked her head to the side, and Renee realized she would have to say something.

"How's your hand?"

Max looked down and held out her hand, flexing the fingers a few times. The knuckles were scraped and pink. "Fine," she said.

"Good. I'm glad." They fell silent again. Renee looked down at her shoes, which caused her to see Max's socks. They were old, dingy, and the elastic had gone out causing them to pool around her ankles. Renee looked away, facing out of the alley again. "I'm not sure why I came."

Max just kept staring. It was unnerving.

"I shouldn't have been in that alley last night. I was... it was stupid. If you hadn't been there, I'm not sure..." She wished she could finish one of these sentences, any of them. She pressed her lips together and tugged on the lapels of her coat. "I don't like being afraid. I keep people at a distance. I worry about people... knowing where I am, where I live. I hide. I'm so fucking sick of hiding."

She hadn't realized she was going to say any of this, but she suddenly realized it had been the real purpose of her entire morning.

"Last night I realized what it might be like if I didn't have to be afraid anymore. I-I want to feel like that all the time, and I think the only way that's possible is if you're always nearby."

"I'm not a bodyguard."

"You did a decent impression of one last night. I talked to the man downstairs, and it sounds like you might be on the verge of getting kicked out. I'm positive I can double whatever he's been paying you. And I have a guest house in my backyard."

Max snorted and looked over her shoulder into the apartment.

"I'm living in a storage closet, and you... you have a house you aren't using."

Renee winced. "It's not really a house. It doesn't have a bathroom. But there's a... a guest bath in the house you could use if you moved in."

"Are you fucking serious about this? You just show up out of the blue and offer me a job and a place to live? You don't know me. I could be a junkie. I could be an alcoholic asshole. People don't end up living above a boxing gym because they make consistently great life choices. What the hell could possibly make you feel safe about inviting me into your home?"

"You walked away," Renee said. "And then you came back."

Max snorted and shook her head. She smacked her hand against the door a few times, pushing her jaw out as she considered the proposal. Finally she looked back into the apartment and stood up straighter.

"You're right about my employment in this shithole. And my prospects at continued residency in this apartment. Costello will be glad to see the back of me, and I'm already looking forward to never cleaning another men's room again." She let go of the door and retreated inside. "Come on in. I'll pack some shit and we can go right now."

Renee was surprised but stepped over the threshold. She'd expected to give Max her address and they would arrange a time for her to come look at the guest house. She didn't expect an immediate tenant. But looking around the room, she could see why Max wouldn't need very long to vacate the premises. There was a bed under the window, ratty curtains hanging open behind broken blinds. One chair, a couch, and a table next to a closet without a door.

Max already had a suitcase open on the bed and was shoving clothes into it without pausing to fold them. She had at least taken the time to pull on a pair of black jeans with rips in both knees.

"I appreciate this," Renee said. "We can discuss the, um, finer details of... of what's expected of you once you're settled."

"Sure," Max said. "So what the hell do you do? Spare guest house, hiring me as a live-in whatever, plus those boots cost more than anything in this apartment."

Renee smiled skeptically. "You don't know?"

"How would I? I don't think you even told me your name."

"I did. It's Renee Lamar."

"Oh. Right." She straightened and shrugged. There was a complete lack of recognition in her eyes. "You are beautiful. So. You're rich, you're beautiful. You're probably an actress. I don't watch TV and I never go to the movies."

Renee couldn't help but smile. "Yes. Yes, I-I'm an actress."

"Oh," Max said. "Famous?"

"Depends on who you—"

"Forget it." Max zipped up her suitcase and looked around for anything she might have forgotten. She went to the fridge and took out three cans of beer dangling from plastic rings. She pulled one free and held it out to Renee. "Want?"

"No..."

Max shrugged and kept it, putting the other two on top of the fridge. "That should cover my back rent. All right, let's get out of here."

"Don't you need to... quit? Or let Costello know where you're going?"

"Fuck him." Max lifted her suitcase off the bed with one hand, letting it thump to the floor. She wheeled it past Renee. She walked out into the sunshine without looking back.

She was halfway down the stairs before she shouted back, "Come on, let's go if we're going."

Renee stood in the apartment and tried to wrap her head around what had just happened. She'd come here with no goals or intentions. But planned or not, she had to be hopeful it would turn out well. And if she had come here with no expectations, then it couldn't be said that it had gone poorly.

She pushed her hair out of her face and followed her new tenant down the stairs.

CHAPTER THREE

"ANTIMATTER IS *a sci-fi film that would prefer to be horror, but forgets to be frightening. Jump scares and gore take the place of anything resembling coherent thought. The cast is reduced to victims of a director with no vision or finesse, lost to run through poorly-lit corridors and stare in unconvincing terror at a green screen. Renee Lamar sure can scream, though.*"

Max didn't think about the fact she hadn't showered until they were already out of the apartment. She looked back at the actress, who was following her down the stairs. "Do you have a car?"

"I took an Uber."

"I'll drive," Max said, facing forward again. If the smell was noticeable, she would just blame it on the car. "You can navigate."

"Excellent."

The other woman sounded wary, maybe regretting how quickly everything had happened up in the apartment. Max decided to give her a way to get out of it.

"I don't expect to set down roots immediately. If it turns out your little guest house is too cramped, there's no obligation for me to stick around. Same goes for you. If you decide this was a huge mistake, you can tell me to get lost."

Renee said, "I won't just kick you out on the street."

"Wouldn't be the first time."

Max was parked at the far end of the block, away from any spots which might be taken by clients of the gym. That rule meant she had to walk past a dozen empty spaces before arriving at her car. She didn't have to look to know Renee was regarding the car with dismay and regret. It was a '68 Plymouth Sport Satellite, once a classic but not so much anymore. She'd bought the shell and spent a few years turning it into a viable mode of transportation. That was about all it could be called. It wasn't reliable, it wasn't pretty, and no one would call it a classic. But she was proud of it, despite how trashy it looked. Or maybe because of its distressed state. This was her car, and there wasn't another exactly like it anywhere in the world.

She threw her bag into the back and waited until Renee was in the passenger seat before she started the engine. It burped, grunted, and settled into a low but steady murmur.

"Which way am I heading?"

Renee nodded forward. "Take the PCH north. Pacific Palisades."

Max arched an eyebrow. "Wow. You were pretty far from home last night."

"So were you."

Max accepted that as an answer and drove. When they were at stoplights, she casually looked at her passenger, who was too distracted by her own thoughts to notice the attention. The lady was probably famous and, while Max doubted she'd seen any of her movies, she must have seen a poster or an advertisement for something. Renee had a unique profile - her regal nose was a perfectly smooth curve, her lips were full, and she had a powerful cleft chin. Her jaw was could have been carved in marble, at least the part of it which wasn't concealed by the red hair pinned under the collar of her coat. Her eyes were the loveliest feature, though. Bright, bright blue, shadowed by makeup to create the illusion of depth beneath barely-there brows.

But while the woman was undeniably beautiful, gorgeous even, Max couldn't remember ever seeing this profile on a bus stop or billboard.

"So what have you been in? Superhero shit?" She shrugged. "Not that I'm judging, by the way. I know everything is superheroes these days. I like comic books."

Renee laughed and ducked her head. "You're not wrong. And

yes, I actually have done a superhero movie. It was based on a book called *Luce Kanon*." She paused, and Max shrugged, shaking her head. "Well. I try not to get pigeon-holed. I mostly do smaller movies. Indies that go out to film festivals and get a small cult following. I do the bigger movies so I can afford to take a few months off for the smaller jobs that really mean something."

Max said, "Huh." She had a feeling the paycheck for the 'smaller' movies was still more than she would see in a year of paychecks, but she didn't say that.

"Take a right up here," Renee said. "Do you have GPS? I could just put my address into that."

"I don't like them. People forget how to move around on their own, and when their phone dies or the wifi goes out, they're lost. Literally and figuratively."

Renee said, "Wow. You're too young to be that scared of technology."

"Maybe I'm just old enough to remember when people didn't have the answer to everything in their pocket. What's your best friend's phone number? How do I get home from work? We built a safety net and we only keep ourselves sane by not thinking about what would happen if it got taken away."

Renee said, "Wow. Okay. So no GPS. Got it. Do you at least have a phone?"

Max grimaced. "Yeah, I have a phone. It's the twenty-first century, I can't not have a phone."

"Well that's something, at least.

Renee smiled as she turned to look out the window again. There was a chuckle in her voice, but Max didn't get the impression she was being mocked or laughed at. Renee let the silence linger until the next stop light.

"It's not always a safety net. Technology, I mean." She wet her lips and kept her eyes cast down. Her voice was softer now, more contemplative. "Sometimes it can be a straitjacket."

"No one's forcing you to put it on."

"Yeah," Renee said. "But it's scarier without it."

Renee used terse, simple instructions to take them the rest of the way home. "A right," off the Pacific Coast Highway, then a left, and another left onto a winding road made claustrophobic by trees, hedges, and retaining walls meant to block out prying eyes from the properties on the other side. And then suddenly everything fell away on both sides, revealing bright blue skies to her right and a spectacular and completely unobstructed ocean vista to the left. The road was on the edge of a lush green cliff which plummeted straight down to the beach.

"It's the second house here."

"Wait, here?" She'd indicated a house positioned so that the ocean seemed to be part of her front yard. "*This* is where you live?"

"Most of the time," Renee said.

Max pulled into the driveway. The house was the same slate grey as the stone steps leading up to the porch. Some effort had been taken to provide color with plants on the curved steps leading up to the front door, and the desert of her actual front yard was decorated with stones and verbena. The roof of the garage was a patio, and she could see a pair of lounge chairs and a closed umbrella. The front of the house was dominated by a large picture window because of course it was, why pay for a house like this and then block out the view?

"This is where you live?" Max said again.

"Yes," Renee said, as if she understood and was annoyed by the question at the same time. "Would you like to stay out here for a while to ogle the view? Most people do the first time they visit."

Max said, "No, that's... no."

She got her bag out of the backseat and followed Renee up the steps. She did look back, amazed at the expanse behind them. How could anyone live with a view like that? Renee hadn't even glanced over as they came around the curve and, as far as Max could tell, hadn't looked back once after they were parked. How could anyone get so jaded that they barely even noticed a view like this? She supposed if things went well, she was likely to find out.

The front door opened into a spacious and spartan living room, which was sunken slightly from the attached dining room. Renee punched a code into the security system to silence its warning chimes, then stepped into the space and swept a hand across it like a game show hostess.

"If you decide to stay, you'll be more than welcome to use the main house. You'll probably have to use the kitchen... the one out in the guest house isn't very well appointed."

"I can probably make do."

"Regardless, feel free." She pointed down a hallway as she continued toward the patio doors between the kitchen and dinner table. "Your bathroom is down there, first door on the right. It has a shower, tub, whatever you may need. Right this way. I'll show you to the guest house."

The backyard was a postage stamp of desert between a small pool on one side and the guest house on the other. The space between them was about the size of garden only with stones, ferns, and a few more bright purple flashes of verbena. The guest house itself looked like a pre-fab shack - a door with curtained windows on either side - and it was nicer than anywhere Max had called home in the past few years. Renee unlocked the door and ushered her inside.

"There's an entrance through the garage, so you can keep your own schedule without worrying about me checking up on you. But like I said, you'll be more than welcome in the house."

"Lots of stuff in there I could steal," Max said. "You're handing me the keys to the castle here and just trusting I won't rob you blind."

Renee shrugged. "I suppose. But after what happened last night, I decided I needed to put my faith in someone. And I felt that the person who stepped in and saved me deserved some sort of compensation. Whether that's permanent or just a week or two living in my guest house, whether it means I have to buy a new laptop and cancel all my credit cards, I thought it was worth the risk."

Max shrugged and nodded.

"For now, settle in. We'll have dinner tonight around five o'clock and we can discuss the fine print of the arrangement. I'll see you then."

She walked past Max and left, closing the door behind her.

Max stood where she was and slowly examined her new, possibly temporary home. It was about the same size as her apartment, maybe a bit smaller, but the details made all the difference. The panel bed seemed massive, crowding into the living room. The kitchen and dining room spanned the far wall, separated by a counter.

Max was no stranger to sudden and unexpected upheavals. After the Miriam Rudd debacle, she'd avoided going home because of all the reporters lurking outside. Every idiot with a camera wanted to get a shot of her to do a profile about the aftermath, to shout questions at her from across the street, to try and make her relive the worst night of her life so they could translate it into clicks and views. They wanted to dig the knife a little deeper, make her bleed, and everyone who read about it with their morning coffee would forget about it when they read lunchtime's breaking story.

Renee probably understood that feeling all too well. It was probably worse for her. Max only had to worry about one cataclysmic newsworthy event. For a celebrity, every errand she ran was potentially newsworthy.

She picked up her suitcase and put it on the kitchen table, opened it, so she could put away the food she'd brought from her apartment. Even the refrigerator was more spacious than the one she'd left behind. Her condiments and beers looked puny and pathetic with acres of available shelf space surrounding them.

Max wandered out of the main room and discovered the only other rooms were a small bathroom next to a windowless space that included a washer and dryer. She wondered if this was for her use or if doing Renee's laundry would be part of her residency requirements. She would probably find out at dinner.

She went back to the main room and sat on the foot of the bed. It wasn't where she'd planned to be when she woke up that morning, and her prospects had been considerably brightened by the offer. She would have to surrender some measure of privacy, of course, and she didn't know how often she would be called upon to protect Renee. Was the previous night's scuffle an aberration or the status quo? That was something else she would have to ask about at dinner.

She squeezed her hand into a fist and looked down at the knuckles. Still red, still sore. It had felt good to punch someone again, to hit with a purpose, to fight for more than just the sake of release

Maybe this arrangement could work out, maybe it would be a disaster for both of them. Still, she felt it was worth a shot.

One pill, washed down with a mouthful of water. That was all Renee really needed to take the edge off. Crushing them up and snorting them the night before had been the result of desperation rather than a change to the status quo. She was a little anxious about taking one with a complete stranger in the house, but she could claim it was an aspirin if she was caught. And she absolutely needed something to take the edge off after this bizarre turn of events.

She had no idea what she'd been thinking. She'd realized on the ride home that she didn't even know Max's last name. She only knew her first name because Costello had told her. Maybe it was a case of temporary insanity. Maybe it was a side effect of snorting the pills instead of swallowing them. Whatever her reasoning, or lack thereof, she now had a stranger nesting in the guest house. She didn't regret the decision, she just wanted an after-action report to see how she had ended up like this.

From the kitchen counter, she could crane her neck and see the front door of the guest house. Usually she ignored it, but now it felt ominous. This woman, this Max Doe, could peek in on her most intimate moments. She'd put so much effort into her privacy and now she'd drilled a peep hole into the wall of her home. She stepped around the counter and lowered the blinds, casting the room into shadows but making her feel slightly better about the intruder.

They would get to know each other over dinner, and they could decide together if they wanted to go through with this bizarre experiment. Until then she would just hide out inside. She went back to the kitchen and took another pill, washing it down with the rest of her water.

It was just to calm her nerves. It was a very unusual day, she'd been dangerously close to withdrawals, and she was just trying to balance herself out.

Nothing to worry about, she was certain.

CHAPTER FOUR

"THERE'S NOTHING *really new about the framework of* Holly's Holding it Together. *A similar story is probably playing out on three basic cable channels as you read this. Writer-director Molly Koenig's film is truly held together by a star-making performance by Renee Lamar, who makes her presence known from the first frame and doesn't let you look away until well after the final credits start rolling.*"

Renee decided that the best way to ignore the interloper she'd invited into her home was to just pretend she wasn't there. She opened her laptop and checked her phone while it booted up. Two messages from her agent, Lillian, asking her to please call back about the scripts she was supposed to be reading. She'd read them both and really couldn't care less which role she was stuck in. A Benedict Arnold movie, where she would play his wife, or a modern-day action movie where she would get one fight while the lead, an actor in his mid-fifties, got the actual characterization. The only thing she cared about was where the movies filmed. Beyond that, she was just one more well-dressed lamp on one more set.

But she still had to make a choice, so she pulled up one of the scripts at random and skimmed them. The Benedict Arnold movie had more substance than she expected, painting his wife Peggy Shippen as a Lady Macbeth who orchestrated her husband's treason. It would film in Virginia, which would at least save her the trouble of passports and international travel. She checked the action movie - the seventh in a franchise which had already introduced and discarded four female leads in its past installments - and saw that it would film in Budapest and Andalusia.

"Never been to Spain," she murmured, tapping her finger on the keyboard before she went back to the first script. After reading through the first act, she dialed Lillian's number.

"Lillian Swikert."

"It's Renee."

The professional shine fell off the other woman's voice. "It's about damn time. Have you made a decision? I have both studios breathing down my neck for an answer by last week."

"Is the nudity absolutely necessary in the Benedict Arnold one?"

"You know they always believe it's necessary. But I can ask." There was a typing sound as she made a note. "You haven't read the whole script for *Crush and Crash*, have you?"

Renee said, "No, why? What did I miss?"

"Gratuitous lesbian kiss during the villain fight."

Renee rolled her eyes. "Of course there is. Okay, then I guess I'm definitely doing *Benedict*."

"That's not the name anymore. I guess they're worried people will think it's a biopic about that Cumberbatch guy. Now it's called *To the Inhabitants of America*."

"Whatever. Tell them I'll do it. When does filming start?"

"Next year sometime. April, I think. I'll send you the official days when I have them. So how are things going with you?"

Renee glanced toward the back windows. Of all her acquaintances, Lillian was the most likely to understand what Renee had done. They'd been friends since college, and knew everything about each other. Lillian was the one who found Renee's first provider - their chosen word for the person who sold her pills, since every other job title sounded seedy and awful - but even so, this seemed like something she couldn't share. Not yet. Not while it was still so potentially temporary.

"Nothing. Just going crazy in this house."

"Crazy enough to finally sit down and make a decision," Lillian said. "I won't complain about that kind of crazy. But if you need to get out, get some fresh air, breathe, I can probably find a place where you can spend an evening with free alcohol and appetizers."

Renee said, "I'm not that desperate yet. But keep me in mind if anything can't-miss comes up."

"I'll get my feelers up. And I'll call Greg to ask about the nudity. If he won't change it..."

"I'm still in," Renee said, "but I wanted to ask."

Lillian said, "Yep, understood. I'll get back to you when I have an answer. Anything else you need, babe?"

"Nope, everything's good here."

"Everything go okay last night?"

Renee thought again about telling her the truth, but Lillian would overreact. She would insist on a change in procedure, ban Renee from going out to get her own pills... Renee didn't want that.

"It went fine, but I'd prefer not to go back to that part of town again."

"Yeah, no one wants to go there. But you know, short notice and desperate measures. You got what you needed?"

"Everything's a-okay."

Lillian said, "Good. I worry about you."

What'd you say, bitch? His hand tightening around her wrist, his face instantly changing from 'we're friends and I'm giving you a hard time' to something much darker, much more dangerous. His grip felt unbreakable and her mind had gone blank. She couldn't see a way to make him let go, no way out of the beating that suddenly seemed inevitable.

"There's nothing to worry about."

She heard a door close on the other side of the line, and Lillian's voice became even softer. "I'm going to say this again: let me provide for you."

"Lili, I appreciate--"

"No one would know who it's for. There would be layers of protection between you and the source. I've done it before and I'll do it again. Just one of the many services I provide."

Renee said, "I'll keep it in mind."

"That's all I can ask. I'll get back to you when Greg gets back to me."

"Thanks."

She hung up and put her phone down, sliding it across the counter so it would be just out of reach so she wouldn't be tempted to pick it up and poke around. That was never wise or safe. Too many people on the internet with too much access. Information spread around a hive mind, and everyone had their opinions with no shame about sharing them, and the phone would let her hear every word they said if she chose to listen.

Then again. Sometimes it was good to know what people were saying, if they were saying anything.

Her mind was fuzzy enough from her latest dose that she stretched across the counter, retrieved the phone, and opened Twitter. She had an official account which was maintained by some intern at Lillian's office, but she also had a secret account nobody knew about. Her name there was Jules Morgan, a name chosen completely at random. She occasionally tweeted about movies or TV shows. Nothing scandalous, just venting things she could never say in public in case she was ever hired for the show or had to work with anyone involved with it.

She searched for her name and received a column of tweets. There were screenshots of her in various movies - 2013's romcom *Chasing Grace* and 2011's horror movie *Bedlam* seemed to be the most popular this month - and random tabloid shots of her walking off sets. A few people shared links of last month's appearance on *The Tune*. Then there were the people who had apparently peaked in high school and took their catty gossip to social media.

"Can't watch Renee Lamar movies anymore. CGI eyebrows onto this poor ginger!"

"Sometimes I wonder why I don't watch more Renee Lamar movies. Then she speaks and I'm like oh right."

"renee lamar looks like someone put a wig on a lizard lol"

"*In the Pocket*, 2015. 43:32. Renee Lamar: bare tits."

"I would say Renee Lamar is a alien in disguise but it don't even bother to try lookin human. FREAKY EYES"

She realized she was touching her eyebrows as she scrolled. She stopped and curled her fingers against her palm, sitting up straighter and pushing the phone away again. She'd always been sensitive about her eyebrows and her 'unique' looks, but those looks had been part of why she started getting hired for roles. Directors called her exotic, they said she had a 'timeless essence,' and sure enough, her first big roles had been for movies set in the forties and fifties. With the right hairdo, she could be a housewife straight out of a Norman Rockwell painting. Stick her in a leotard and slick her hair back, and suddenly she looked right at home on a starship.

Now that she was famous, those looks were fair game for anyone on the internet to judge and mock. It hadn't helped that one of her earliest films had her playing a woman who turned into a fish monster. She had a wide mouth and deep-set eyes, so the prosthetics had only enhanced what was already there. She hadn't thought through the repercussions of pointing out the piscine bone structure which was first brought to her attention in high school.

She scrolled her thumb down the screen, eyes skimming across the short, terse judgements. There was also praise, but those occasionally veered too close to stalker territory for her to take too much pride in them. She worried her bottom lip with her teeth and narrowed her eyes. "Weird," one person said. "Ugly," claimed another. "Can't act, never liked her much, who is she banging to get~"

Renee knew she should turn off the phone and forget the internet existed. These were anonymous, angry people, most of whom weren't even brave enough to put their own face on their accounts. People paid millions to have her in their movies. People paid money to see her on the big-screen. She knew that for every person shouting about how much they hated her, there were two or five or ten more who liked her. She knew that reading these comments was just pouring salt into a wound that would heal if she just let it alone.

She kept scrolling.

Max stared at the wall. If she held her breath, she could hear the ocean. It sounded like trucks on the freeway, a sound she'd become well-acquainted with as a child. On the road with her mother, moving from city to city, a new bed in a new hotel every night. Mama wanted to be a rock star so she toted her guitar and everything else they owned in the back of a camper down the highways to whatever dive bar was willing to pay her to sing.

Some guys tried to back out of the agreement and pay her in beer. "I can't feed my daughter with free beer. Pay me what you promised." Sometimes they tried to get her to provide another service in exchange for the cash. Max only saw these interactions through the slats of a swinging door that led into a kitchen. Mama would let them take her back there, out of sight, and then she'd kick the back of his knee to drop him down, chop him where his neck met the shoulder to deaden one arm, and grab the hand he reached out to grab her with. She did something with her fingers - always so small against the meaty paw - and pinched between the thumb and forefinger. "My money," she'd say, and she wouldn't let go until her other hand was full of bills.

Then they would run. Back to the hotel, into the camper, on the road again before the bartender tracked her down. She didn't even stop to make sure it was the right amount. Sometimes it was, more often they shorted her, and they ended up losing money on the gig.

Max's mother was the first fighter she'd ever seen in real life. Max was fourteen, and they were outside of a town in Alabama that didn't deserve a name, sleeping in the camper because they hadn't earned enough for a hotel that week, when she asked Mama to teach her how to fight. "You keep bringing me to these bars where you're working," Max said, "and I'm not a little girl anymore. Pretty soon those drunks are going to start noticing. It would be nice if I was able to defend myself."

It wasn't exactly training. They would spar whenever they had a chance, and Mama would give her tips. Max learned how to anticipate and neutralize an opponent's attacks. She learned how it felt to hit and be hit. People were precious about their bodies and hated pain. Fights could be ended so quickly just by scaring people into thinking they would be hurt worse if they didn't back off.

She was seventeen the day she punched her mother hard enough to knock her out. When Mama blinked her eyes back into focus from a prone position on the floor, she slapped Max on the cheek in an affectionate way and laughed.

"I think at this point you're just kicking my ass. We may have to rethink this."

At their next stop, Max went out and found a biker club a few miles away from the bar where her mother was singing. She asked the bartender about any boxing competitions where she could earn some money and within half an hour, he'd found an opponent. A hundred bucks if she stayed upright for five minutes. Five hundred for ten minutes. A thousand if she somehow dropped her opponent. They cleared an area in the game room and she faced off against a burly guy with a stained white shirt stretched across his chest and tattoos ringing his forearms.

She almost lost on the first blow. No surprise, a biker hit harder than Mama. But she managed to stop her stumble before it turned into a fall. She brought her fists back up.

"Nah, I ain't doing this again," he said. "That felt real wrong."

"Come on," she said, "you back out, I still get the five hundred just for standing up. Make it hard for me."

"I'll make it hard for you!" someone shouted.

Her opponent shook his head and tried to back out. Max moved to block him and bopped him on the head with her fist.

"Gonna walk away from a fight with a girl?"

"This is no-win for me, sweetheart, sorry. Look, you're that hard up for cash, maybe you can earn it a nicer way, huh?"

Max punched him in the face. "Coward."

He clapped a hand over his nose. "What the hell are you doing?"

"Going for the thousand," she said, punching him again. "Come on, you pussy, fight back."

She could see his anger rising. "Lady..."

Max swung again. He blocked her out of instinct and, in the same motion, punched her in the side of the head. She reeled and recovered, only to be greeted by another punch. He seemed to have realized the only way out of this was to put her down. Good. She fought back, landed a few more solid blows, but eventually he got her good enough that she spun on the ball of her foot and collapsed into a table. Someone helped her up and put an ice pack in her hand.

When the throbbing went down, the bartender turned her other hand palm up on the bar. He counted five hundred dollar bills into it. "Jonah kept track. Ten minutes and eight seconds." He added another five bills. "Because if anyone asks, it didn't happen here."

She nodded - which caused her brain to scream inside her skull - and closed her hand around the money.

Her mother was already in the hotel room when she got back. Her eyes widened and her jaw dropped when she saw Max's face, and her anger was replaced with confusion when she saw the wad of money Max was holding. They stood silently staring at each other for a long time as Mama put the clues together and realized what had happened.

"Stitches?" she finally said.

"No, I don't think so."

Mama worked her jaw and nodded at the money. "How much."

"A grand."

"God. That'll help a lot..."

"I know."

Max put the money on the bed and went to clean herself up in the bathroom.

After that, their trips had two goals. Find a place where Mama could sing, and scour the outskirts of town for places where Max could earn some money of her own. Mama hated it, but she couldn't deny how helpful the money was. She invested in a first-aid kit and learned how to tend the various wounds her daughter came back with.

"You really want to make money this way?" Mama asked the night Max broke her nose. "This seems like a valid career path for you?"

"I'm good at it."

"I'd hate to see if you sucked at it."

But Max was good, even the guys who kicked her ass admitted that much. She was just outmatched in size and stamina. One bartender who helped her up and put an ice pack against her cheek said, "You're always gonna be smaller than them. But stamina is something you can work at. Ask their wives how long these guys can last before they're huffing and puffing. Get to where you can go ten minutes without breaking a sweat, you'll have a real chance."

She took his advice. She started training and soon she could hold her own with any man in any bar. All she had to do was run out the clock. She got better at avoiding their fists, because she quickly learned that drunken men all seemed to have the same sloppy fighting style. By the time she was twenty, she could finish a fight without getting hit once. She started boxing in amateur tournaments for the challenge and because they were bigger paychecks, and soon she was making a name for herself.

That was the same year she and Mama went their separate ways. Max was an adult, and decided it was time to make her own way in the world. She applied for a professional boxing license, found a manager, and was scheduled for her first bout at an Oklahoma casino. Mama broke her rule about not attending Max's fights to watch her professional debut, a fight against a local woman named Kennedy Collingwood. Max started strong but faltered early and never recovered. Collingwood won in a knockout.

Later, in the locker room, Mama found her being tended to by a ring physician. She waited until the man was gone, leaning against the doorway with her arms crossed over her chest. It was dark in the locker room, and Mama's hair hung over her face so that her expression was shadowed and unreadable.

"This is what you want to do for a living? Be hit and hit back?"

"It's what I'm good at."

Mama rolled her shoulders and flipped her hair back out of her face. She nodded sagely. "Well, I'd be a pretty big hypocrite if I turned into my mother. 'don't you dare go out on the road and play your music, that girl needs a stable home.' Maybe that's why you're making this choice. But whatever happens, I support you." She held out her hand. "Good luck, little girl."

Max shook her mother's hand. It was a very polite and professional parting of the ways, but Max didn't even think it was odd until much later when she was falling asleep on her manager's couch. No hug, no tears, not even waving to each other as the camper pulled out of the parking lot. They were on their own roads. Maybe one day their paths would cross again but for the time being, Max had become someone else. She wasn't going to be a tagalong daughter anymore.

She was Max "Wrecker" Reszke, and she was a fighter.

CHAPTER FIVE

"A FORTUNATE *side effect of* Wind Advisory *languishing in reshoots is a surprise appearance by Renee Lamar, who appears in only one brief scene before sacrificing screen time to far more inferior actors. The underuse of a talent like Lamar is just one of countless missteps on this trouble production.*"

Max wasn't aware of when she'd fallen asleep, but at some point she had fallen back onto the bed and drifted off. The mattress was the softest she'd slept on in months, maybe years, and her body surrendered to it. The purple-pink light coming through the window told her that several hours had passed while she was unconscious, meaning she'd lost an entire day. But it hardly mattered if she now had a place to stay without fear of eviction. She didn't have to worry about where her next dollar was coming from or if her bank account was gathering dust. Maybe that was part of the reason she'd fallen into such a deep and unbroken sleep; letting go of all that stress had turned her brain off.

She sat up and ran a hand through her hair. She wondered if Renee's invitation to wander the grounds was authentic. It felt awkward to leave the pool house, like she was a pet that had been brought home and shown to her cage. She stood and went to the door, paused when she heard movement in the backyard but finally twisted the knob and stepped outside.

A table next to the pool was set for two. She was fairly sure it hadn't been there when Renee showed her around. As if cued, Renee came out of the house with a camping lantern in one hand and a bottle of wine in the other. She stopped when she saw Max.

"Oh. I knocked but you didn't answer. I thought you might have been in the shower or..."

Right, a shower. Max realized she could probably use one of those. "Fell asleep." She nodded at the table. "I can close the blinds and play my music loud if you're getting ready for a date or something."

"No, this is for you. Us. I thought we could have our conversation over a nice meal." She put the wine down. "Combination business meeting and welcoming you to the house. If you decide to stay."

"Okay," Max said slowly. "Do I have time to take a shower?"

"Sure." Renee took out her phone. "Food is supposed to be delivered in twenty-five minutes, so you should be safe."

Max nodded. "Okay. I'll be right back."

She went back into the pool house and leaned against the door. Was she really going to have dinner next to a shining pool, in the Pacific Palisades, in a mansion across the street from a magnificent ocean view? Maybe this was all some hallucination... No. She had suffered concussions and she knew the symptoms. They didn't include delusions. Of course, they might be a result of some other traumatic brain injury. Maybe she was standing on Hollywood Boulevard right now talking to a movie poster, imagining the movie star was some kind guardian angel who had swept down to lift her out of the gutter.

She didn't know how to test reality without hurting herself. Maybe the shower would help. She went into the small bathroom, stripped quickly, and stepped into the stall. The cold water hit her in the face like a slap, sending shockwaves down her spine all the way out to her fingertips and toes. She bowed her head to let the water flatten the stuck-up spikes of her hair and cascade over her neck. The tub remained solid under her feet. She put her arms straight out in front of her, palms flat on the tile, and the texture didn't change to a brick wall.

"Okay," she said. "Okay. So this is happening. This is all really happening."

Max straightened and cupped her hands under the water. It

was warm now. The shower at her apartment over Costello's rarely had hot water for longer than two minutes. She splashed her face, scrubbed, lathered up, scrubbed again, and tried not to think about the gorgeous woman waiting for her outside. *This is for you. Us.* Surely nothing to read into there. No subtext. Just a business transaction that happened to take place over food.

The water was still hot. She planned to stay in the shower until it went cold or she figured out which of her wrinkled and unwashed outfits she was supposed to wear to dinner with a movie star.

Renee paid the delivery driver - smiling at his unblinking stare as she handed over his tip - and took the bags out so she could set the table. She'd spent the day considering how to move forward. Eventually she decided that this dinner would decide the professional/personal boundary between her and Max. If they hit it off, they could be friendly. If Max acted like an employee, she could just as easily assume the role of boss. She had no real preference, but it would be good to set the boundaries early.

She had taken a seat and finished pouring the wine when Max reappeared. She had changed into a blue dress shirt in need of ironing and black jeans. An attempt had been made with a black necktie, but the knot was loose and the top button was undone. Her hair was slicked back out of her face, but it made her look much more threatening. Renee felt a bit out of place in a sheath dress, but she reminded herself it was her home and covered the discomfort with a smile.

"I hope fish is okay. We didn't really discuss dietary restrictions."

"It's fine." Max took a seat across from her and looked at the plate. Her eyes seemed to take in every detail of the table, then shifted to look at the pool. It was lit from below so the water seemed to shimmer. She lifted her chin and looked at the house, then finally rested her attention on Renee. She managed a weak smile, which Renee returned.

"First things first," Renee said. "I don't even know your full name. We should probably start from there."

"Maxine Reszke."

"But you prefer Max."

"Yeah."

Renee nodded. "Okay. That's a good starting point. It's good to officially meet you, Max."

She picked up her glass and held it out. Max looked at it, then looked at her own. Renee could almost see the wheels spinning in her head as she realized what was expected of her. She cupped the bottom of the glass, two fingers on either side of the stem, and brought it up to awkwardly bump it against the side of Renee's. The sound it made was flat and hollow, but it was better than nothing. Max put the glass down and shifted in her seat.

"I'm not used to this sort of thing," she said suddenly. "Obviously. So if I do something stupid, just tell me. I don't want to stand there looking like a moron while everyone snickers behind my back."

"Noted," Renee said.

"So."

"Of course. The job." She unfolded a napkin and draped it over her lap. "After what happened last night, I realized I had spent far too long being afraid. Afraid of people knowing where I live, finding me, taking advantage of me in any number of ways. I take Ubers and have them drop me off half a mile away so they won't see my home. I use fake names for every app that asks for too much information. I have walls between me and the entire world. You made me realize that I don't need walls. I need a shield."

Max had started eating in the middle of the speech. When Renee paused, Max sat up straighter and leaned back in her chair. She finished chewing before she spoke.

"You want me to be a... shield."

"I wouldn't need all the walls if I had protection. I wouldn't need rideshare or delivery services if I had someone who could take me places or pick things up for me. And if I went out and someone tried to hurt me, it would be nice to know I had someone watching my back. In exchange for this service, you would be given a reasonable fee as well as room and board here, in the pool house. If we get along, we could occasionally have dinner like this. If we hate each other, you could stay out there and never see me until I needed you for something."

Max thought about that. "So I'd be a... butler? Assistant?"

"I don't think there's a title that fits everything I'm asking from you. Assistant would probably be closest. Butler implies a level of subservience I don't want or expect. You would be my employee, but you would have complete autonomy. If you think I'm being unreasonable, you would have free rein to call me a bitch."

"Huh." Max poked the rice around the plate with the tines of her fork. "I'm not going to clean your pool or do your laundry."

"No, of course not. I have someone who does that."

"Of course you do." Max took a deep breath and squared her shoulders. "Is that what you do? Collect people? Pay them to hang around and provide you with services?"

Renee didn't know if Max expected her to get defensive in response, but she seemed surprised by Renee's nod.

"Yes. Isn't that what we all do? Uber and Lyft and DoorDash have all made fortunes based on the premise that we all want to hire people to do things we ought to be able to do ourselves. Having money equals convenience. It would be foolish not to use it."

"Fair enough," Max said.

"In a few months, I'll most likely be traveling to Georgia to film a movie. If you're still around at that time, you can decide whether you want to accompany me or remain here. If you come with me, I will cover travel expenses. Flight, hotel, et cetera. Your job on-set would be the same as it is here."

"Shield."

"Exactly."

Max tapped her fork against the plate. Her face was utterly still, completely unreadable. Renee would have hated to play poker against her. Instead of looking for clues to her inner thoughts, she examined the harsh lines of Max's face. There were scars there, old wounds which were still visible in the shape of her brow, her nose, her jaw. This was a woman who had been broken but survived to put herself back together. She was exactly the type of person Renee wanted as her protector, and her pulse raced in the hopes she would agree.

"One condition."

Renee dipped her chin in acknowledgement. "Sure."

"And the chance to add more conditions once I've thought it through."

"Of course."

"You learn how to fight. Krav maga or whatever the trendy thing is these days. You don't have to become a lethal weapon, but I don't want you to be completely helpless out there. I want to know you can hold your own if it takes me a few seconds to get to you."

Renee nodded slowly. "I suppose that makes sense. Does this mean you accept my offer?"

"It means I'll consider it."

"A trial basis," Renee said.

Max shrugged, nodded, and went back to her food.

"You'll have to sign a non-disclosure agreement, no matter what you decide."

"Another shield," Max said.

Renee nodded. "Exactly."

Max shrugged without looking up from her plate. "Sure. Who would I tell?"

"Costello?"

Max laughed and shook her head. "Sure."

"Honestly, there are tabloids who might pay handsomely for something idiotic like the layout of my living room or if I leave comic books laying out."

"Or if I took pictures of you walking around the house in your underwear." She looked up. "Not saying I would do that. I'm just saying I get the threat. I'll sign."

"Thank you."

"And there's nothing shameful about leaving comic books around. Comic books are great."

Renee said, "I know. I got into them when I was researching my superhero movie. They're very addictive."

"Marvel or DC?"

"I don't believe in the rivalry. I think both have great characters, and pretending to ignore one is ridiculous. There are also so many smaller publishers who are doing amazing work."

Max said, "That's a good answer," sounding a little surprised. Renee was a little surprised at herself. She hadn't expected to pontificate on comics, but it was the first time Max had seemed interested in what they were talking about, so she was reluctant to change subjects.

"I might leave some out after all. Feel free to borrow them."

"I might take you up on that."

Renee hid her smile by taking a bite of her food, holding the fork in front of her mouth as she chewed. She liked the metaphor of a shield. She hadn't thought about it before the word came out of her mouth, but it was very apt. She always thought about a suit of armor or a cloak of invisibility to create distance between her and the rest of the world. It was something she'd wanted for so long but she never had a name for it. Now she knew what she needed. She looked at Max's hands, the sharp and scarred knuckles, and hoped she agreed to their arrangement.

She hoped against hope that she had finally found her shield.

CHAPTER SIX

"YOU'VE NO *doubt heard the phrase 'I would watch (actor) read the phone book.' Renee Lamar puts that old adage to the test with Passing Lane, a meandering thriller which never ventures more than fifty yards from a highway. Lamar, this time playing an abductee restrained to the backseat of a Lexus for most of the runtime, still manages to remind us why the word 'Oscar' so often buzzes around her performances.*"

Max signed the non-disclosure agreement the following day. Renee suggested having a lawyer look over it, but Max didn't see the point. She also didn't see the point of negotiating the salary offered in the employment contract. If she was living rent-free and didn't have to worry about paying bills, then she didn't need a fortune. As long as she had enough for gas and groceries, she would be happy. After signing, she went into the house to leave the NDA and contract on the kitchen counter.

She put the papers where they would quickly be spotted and listened to the silent hum of the house. Everything in the kitchen seemed like robots in sleep mode. There was a pair of small, featureless gizmos near the blender which she assumed were voice-activated systems she'd heard so much about, but they didn't seem to be turned on. Beyond it was the spartan living room, smartly decorated but nothing that caught the eye. In fact, most of the house seemed to lack character or flash.

She assumed that was because the real draw was the large picture window that took up most of the living room wall. The front of the house was angled toward the most scenic overlook, and Renee had set up a second seating area there. The three chairs and divan here looked like they would be the most comfortable, which made sense. Max walked into this nook and stared out over the water.

"What the hell am I doing here?" she asked.

"That's an excellent question."

Max tensed and slowly turned toward the speaker. He was handsome, in a weary sort of way, in rumpled clothes and bearing a few days' worth of stubble. He was near the kitchen, which meant he had come from the back of the house rather than the front door, but she doubted he'd been there long. He tilted his head, examining her as she examined him, both sizing the other up for a potential threat. Finally she opted to break the silence.

"I'm Max."

"Max who?"

"I'm... living here. In the guest house. Renee hired me."

He said, "As a pool... boy?"

"It's complicated. Maybe she should explain it."

"Yeah, maybe so." He took out his phone and poked at the screen.

Max moved closer. "Actually, she hired me as protection. She didn't tell me anyone was going to stop by. How do I know you're even supposed to be here."

He turned the phone around so she could see Renee's picture. "I have her number."

"That doesn't prove jack shit. Who are you?"

"Who..." He looked at her again as if reassessing her. "Are you seriously asking that question?"

She shrugged.

"Rand." She stared at him without understanding. "Randall *Hurley*."

She said, "Okay. Rand. Do you have a reason for being in this house?"

He laughed and shook his head. He hit send on his phone and brought it up to his ear. "More of a reason than you do, buddy. Hey," he said into the phone. "It's me. I– no, I'm at your place. Listen– because Matty got hurt so they shut down production for a week. Listen, there's some guy in your house who claims you hired him for protection."

Max snorted and turned her back, wandering back to the picture window.

"No, he said his name was Max... oh. I guess... so you know who she is?" He listened to her. "Did something happen? I'm... yeah. Okay. Yeah... I'll be here. See you then."

Max looked back to see him disconnecting the call. "So everything sorted out?"

Rand didn't look happy. "I suppose so. Look, I'm just going to crash here for a while. I... I don't, uh, I don't know what arrangement you had with Renee, but..."

"I'll stick to the guest house while you're here. I was just dropping off some papers Renee wanted me to sign."

He looked at the counter and nodded. "Well. Okay, then. And, uh, just so you know, Renee is my... I'm..." He sighed heavily and shook his head. "I don't know what we are, but I can assure you, I'm welcome to stay here."

"I figured, since you called her."

"Right. Ah, well, then..."

Max gestured at the back door. Max walked past him and outside, not bothering to look back. She assumed he was another actor, someone she'd never heard of. The little disbelieving raise of his eyebrows when she didn't immediately recognize his name - "Rand," what kind of person shortened Randall to "Rand"? - was something she would probably have to get used to if she was going to spend time with Renee. The expectation of being known was egotistical and enough to instantly put someone on Max's wrong side. She anticipated being introduced to a lot of people who would be angry at her simply because she didn't know who they were.

Working for Renee Lamar would be good money, but it definitely wasn't going to be easy.

Renee resisted the urge to swear as she marched up the driveway like a general on the way to address her troops. Rand had called halfway into her jog, the jangling of his ringtone interrupting the podcast she'd been listening to. She almost ignored it, certain he was just calling from set so they could have phone sex in his trailer, but she answered against her better judgement. Every word out of her mouth had increased her horror, and she'd started running back even before she hung up.

She'd barely been out of the house forty-five minutes and everything went to shit. Why did Rand have to come back today? She wasn't even completely comfortable with the new arrangement yet and now found herself in the position of defending it to someone else. She didn't even know for sure if Max planned to stay.

The front room of the house was empty when she threw open the door. She went directly down the hall to her bedroom, where she found Rand sitting on the foot of her bed in an unbuttoned shirt. He was barefoot and appealingly bedraggled, the sort of handsome dishevelment that usually took an entire wardrobe department to achieve. He had been looking at his phone, but he sat up straighter when she appeared.

"There she is," he said. "You're looking sexy."

She rolled her eyes. She was in black running shorts and long-sleeved top, unwashed hair pulled back in a ponytail. She was dripping sweat, with no makeup, and overheated from racing back to the house. She was sure she was absolutely ravishing. She brushed off the compliment and unzipped her top as she went into the bathroom.

"What are you doing here, Rand?"

"I told you on the phone. Matt got hurt doing a stunt—"

"Yeah, I know why you're not on-set." She turned on the shower and finished undressing, ignoring the fact Rand had followed her and was standing in the bathroom doorway. "What are you doing *here*, instead of at home playing your war games?"

He came into the bathroom. "I wanted to see you. It's been a long time."

"There weren't any lovely young starlets on the set you could take the edge off with?"

He was between her and the towels, so she stared up at him while he ran his eyes over her body. He put his hands on her shoulders and squeezed gently.

"No one makes me feel the way you do, Renee." He was using what he considered his bedroom voice, a low growl that she hated to admit always made her a little weak. "I came all this way."

"I reek. I'm covered with sweat…"

"I don't care."

"*I* care. I'm not going to fuck you when I feel this gross."

He sighed and rolled his eyes. His normal speaking voice returned. "Well, something? I came all this way. Not even a hand job."

It was her turn to roll her eyes. But she figured the best way to end his tantrum was to give in, so she reached for his belt. He smiled and braced one hand on the towel rack, assuming an awkward posture that was so ridiculous she almost laughed. Instead, she licked her fingers went to work. He grunted with appreciation while she focused on the fogged glass window over his shoulder.

"So what's with this, um... Max person...?"

Renee snorted. "Really? You're thinking about her? She's not exactly your type."

"No," he said. "I mean... why is she here? She said you hired her for protection. What do you need protection from?"

"Not your problem."

He was breathing faster now. "It is if... you... are scared for your safety. I could hire a real security firm."

"I don't need your money. Are you almost done?"

"You've got a dangerous hobby," he said, ignoring her question. "I checked your stash. You're running low."

"I have enough." She looked at him again, a line appearing between her eyebrows. She noticed how he was leaning on the towel rack and the shallowness of his breath. She squeezed him and took note of his slow pulse. When he opened his eyes to see why she had slowed down, she saw the pupils were dilated.

"You son of a bitch. How much did you take?"

"Not much..."

She released him, shoving him away from her with the other hand. "Finish yourself off and get out of here. And whatever you took from my stash, I want it back by tomorrow. Understood?"

Rand grunted, cupping his hands protectively in front of himself. "What's the big deal? We dip into each other's stashes all the time!"

"I just... I'm... Replace it, Rand."

She stepped into the shower and pulled the curtain to end the argument. She was aware of him lurking in the bathroom, most likely finishing what she'd started. He was gone by the time she shut off the water. She went back into the bedroom and went directly to her teapot. Rand had taken half of what she'd bought, dropping her back into dire need. He probably took one and kept the rest for later. She slapped her palm on the table top.

"Goddamn it, you damn addict."

She put on a white V-neck and sweatpants before venturing out into the house to confirm he had completely fled the premises. It was lucky he had, since she didn't know what she would have done if she'd found him lurking. She got her phone and sent him a text - "Replace it. ASAP!" - and stormed into the kitchen to get a bottle of water.

She saw the documents on the counter and paused to look over them. Good. Max was apparently sticking around, and the NDA was security she desperately needed right now. If Rand didn't come through, she could just send Max to pick up some more. It was a risk, but a small one, and much less dangerous than going herself.

Rand was a complication she hadn't expected. He was supposed to be off filming for two more months. He wasn't her boyfriend. She wasn't exactly sure what he was. They met four years earlier on a movie called *Hopeless, NV*. He was a local deputy, she was the sheriff's wife, and they were having an affair. The most risqué moment in the movie was when he arrived at their house for a tryst and they were nearly caught in their underwear. Some kissing in lingerie, a bit of over-the-clothes groping, nothing worse than PG-13. At the wrap party, after a few cocktails, he told her he wished it had been a different kind of movie. She asked him to elaborate, and they did a bit of extensive roleplaying in his trailer. A few weeks after that, he called and asked if she wanted to get a drink. She said no, but invited him over anyway.

Since then, they'd been more off than on, to the point where even the most dedicated tabloid had yet to identify them as a couple. She was grateful for that. He was just a guy she fucked, the guy in her bed sometimes when there was no one else taking up the space, and she often wondered if the hassles he brought into her life was worth the occasional night of admittedly great sex.

She'd hoped her arrangement with Max could achieve the same level of anonymity, but Rand ruined that. Maybe it was better that they met like this. Rand had a penchant for showing up in the middle of the night for bootie calls. If Max mistook him for a prowler and attacked him, the police would get involved, and both secrets would be out in the open.

She sighed. So many secrets, so many prying eyes. It was the cost of fame, of doing the job she loved. One day soon, she might have to decide if the reward was worth the price.

CHAPTER SEVEN

"BLOODY DISGUSTING, *truly disturbing, and exquisitely well-done,* Bedlam *is a rebirth for the horror genre. It turns frights into art, and you'll find yourself applauding the beauty onscreen even as you know it will show up in your new nightmares. Renee Lamar stars as a mental patient turned savior who rallies her fellow inmates in a fight for survival with so many twists and turns you'll question every frame of the movie."*

Max opened the door to find Renee standing in front of her with an apologetic smile, freshly showered and looking like a typical soccer mom.

"Sorry about that. Rand is a... friend. He stops by occasionally without warning."

"Just let me know if his invitation is revoked."

Renee nodded. "Will do." Max started to close the door. "Actually..." Max stopped and waited. "If it's not too much trouble, I do need a ride somewhere. If you're not busy."

Max shrugged. "I'm at your beckon call."

Renee said, "Beck *and* call."

"What?"

"It's... you said beckon. It's beck and."

"Beckon makes more sense. What's a beck?"

Renee looked confused. "I'm not sure... But... that's the saying.

It doesn't matter. Um... the ride."

"Yeah. Let me grab my keys."

Renee was waiting by the car when Max came out into the garage, leaning against the hood with her arms crossed over her chest. In her casual suburb outfit and her hair pulled back in a ponytail, she looked like someone's high school sweetheart waiting for him after practice.

"Does that come naturally?" Max asked as she walked around to the driver's side.

"Pardon?"

Max gestured. "Posing. Standing there like you just got cut out of a magazine ad."

"I didn't realize I was doing that. So I suppose it does. Once you've seen a hundred tweets with a picture of yourself mid-sneeze, you get a little self-conscious."

"Huh."

Renee directed her east. "Nine times out of ten, we'll go east when we leave the house. Actually more like nineteen out of twenty. Sometimes I go jogging in Topanga, but otherwise..."

"Noted."

"You don't talk much, do you?"

Max shrugged. "What else needed to be said?"

"I guess you have a point."

"Are we going to be out long?"

Renee said, "I don't think so. It depends on traffic. I just... have to pick something up. Rand took something from my house, and he arranged to have it replaced."

Max nodded. "Is this the same something you were picking up the night we met?"

Renee looked out the window.

"There's only so many reasons someone like you would be meeting a stranger outside that bar. I don't need the details. But if this is another transaction like that, I think maybe I should be the one doing the actual exchange."

"It's Rand's provider. This isn't another back alley situation."

"It doesn't matter. You hired me as a shield, and I intend to serve my purpose."

"Okay. Maybe."

They were silent for the rest of the trip except for when Renee gave directions. This time Max noticed how the neighborhood seemed to be concealed like a fairy tale village. Walls and hills and tall trees were arranged in a way which seemed natural but actually kept away any prying eyes. Pacific Palisades sounded idyllic, but the word meant fortification. The palm trees were named after a fence of iron spikes meant to keep out invaders. In this case, she assumed the invaders would be anyone with less than a million dollars in savings. Now she was on the other side of the palm tree spikes, and she wasn't entirely sure how she felt about that.

They ended up at a row of warehouses surrounded by a fleet of moving vans. Renee told her where to park.

Max said, "You really should stay here. I don't care if this sort of thing happens all the time, I don't think you want some random person on-set recognizing you or what you're picking up."

Renee faced forward and worked her jaw. She looked almost like a child on the verge of a tantrum. But she took a deep breath and slumped back in defeat.

"Fine. You're looking for someone named Zeke Gellar. He's a stuntman. Just ask anyone in there and they should be able to point you in the right direction."

"I'll be back," Max said.

She got out of the car and walked through the open gates into a side lot where people with headsets milled around. She expected some kind of security, but no one paid her more attention than a quick sideways glance before going back to their business. A woman chattering into a walkie-talkie hurried past her, just close enough that Max was able to get in her way.

"Zeke Gellar?"

The woman flipped a hand over her shoulder and continued on her way. Max asked two other people, guided through the maze of vehicles and wardrobe racks standing out in the open air until she found a cluster of trailers. A man in a tight black T-shirt pointed her to a trailer marked as ZEKE with a strip of masking tape on the door. She climbed the metal steps and knocked. A moment later, the door swung open and a string-bean dressed all in black leaned out and glared down at her.

"Whacha?"

She narrowed her eyes. "I'm supposed to pick up something for Renee Lamar."

He leaned out further and looked toward the front of the lot, jutting his unshaven chin out before he pivoted back to look at her. "Whushee?"

"Pardon?"

"Whu," he said slowly. "Rishe."

"Are you asking 'where is she'?" He motioned impatiently. "That's not important. I'm picking it up for her."

The man, presumably Zeke, grunted and swung back into the trailer. He left the door open, so she assumed he was inviting her in. She climbed the steps and waited in the doorway as he went to a backpack on the counter. She didn't know if he was enunciating better or if she had just figured out how to translate him, but the next time he spoke, his words were much clearer.

"Rand said I cuh mee' her, gave'm a discount an' ev'thing. Big discount."

"You'll have to take that up with him," Max said.

He grunted and came back with a pill bottle. "She needs a'thing else, she can come bah tah me. You tell 'er tha'."

"Will do." She took the bottle and slipped it into her pocket.

"Y'ain't gonna count 'em?"

"Nope. Have a nice day."

Max retraced her steps through the lot and arrived back at the car, where she held out the pill bottle as she got behind the wheel.

"You did it," Renee said as she took the bottle and twisted it to look through the clear orange plastic. "Were there any problems?"

"The guy was expecting to meet you. Probably a fan. No big deal." She started the engine. "So. Straight back to the ranch, or is there anything else you need?"

Renee stared at the bottle for another second before she seemed to snap out of her trance. "Yes. The grocery store. We're going to get you something to fill your fridge with."

The offer reeked of charity, and Max balked on principle. "I don't–"

"I saw what you had at your apartment. We'll get you the essentials and take it out of your first paycheck."

Max wanted to argue further, but she really saw no reason to refuse the offer. She sighed and pulled away from the curb.

"Okay. But we're not going to Whole Foods or anyplace where they charge thirty bucks for a jar of olives. We're going to my usual place."

Renee nodded. "Fine."

Max turned away to check traffic, but also to hide her smile at the thought of Renee Lamar wandering the aisles at the Fresh Saver. She might enjoy the errand after all.

Fresh Saver was a warehouse store that didn't waste money on frills, so it ended up feeling less professional than a farmer's market. Produce was barely sorted, and quite a few items were shelved with the price hand-written on unlaminated signage. It was probably more spartan and slapped-together than the loading dock at Whole Foods. Renee stopped at the threshold, her frozen feet holding down the sensor to keep the doors open behind her as Max deposited a quarter to retrieve a cart. She paused and watched Renee take everything in.

"Problem?"

"No," Renee said too quickly. "No, it's fine. Where should we begin?"

Max pointed with her chin. "Cereal. Then veggies. Frozen shit."

"Okay, then."

"Anything you want to veto? Are you vegan?"

Renee said, "We had fish for dinner..."

"Some vegans have fish."

"True. I'm technically vegetarian, except when I'm not. But you have your own kitchenette, so whatever you cook out there is your business. I'm not going to dictate what you eat in your own space."

Max put a box of cereal in her cart. Renee took it out again and examined the ingredients.

"It might not be name brand, but it's the same thing."

"Maybe better." Renee put the box back in the cart. "I wasn't always rich, you know. I've shopped in my fair share of places like this. Granted, it's been a while. But I'm smart enough to know when I'm paying for window dressing. A safer parking lot in a nicer part of town with classical music piped through the ceilings means you pay an extra $2 for a pretty red box and a recognizable name."

Max nodded. "Yep."

Renee smiled. "I can see I'll have to carry the majority of the conversations between us."

"Doesn't seem like it'll be a problem for you."

Renee laughed and ventured forward to the cooler. "Just for that, I'm going to get you almond milk, and you're going to learn to like it."

Shopping was a different experience when she didn't have to worry about price tags or how much money she had in her wallet. She tried not to let her eyes get much bigger than her stomach, but she also bought a few snacks which she wasn't entirely sure she needed but as long as Renee was footing the bill... She watched Renee compare prices between full and half gallons of milk. She took the one which was the better bargain, even if it was a matter of pennies.

"You look like you know what you're doing," Max said.

"Surprised? I once lived on ramen and Kool-Aid. And when I was a kid, grocery shopping was kind of a luxury. Even then, we treated it like a military excursion. We had the list, we got what was on the list, and there was no substituting or improvising. Every penny was accounted for. I think I was fifteen before I understood what an impulse buy was."

"Huh," Max said.

When they got to the checkout, Max took a couple of candy bars off the shelf. She held them up as if they were evidence. "Impulse buy," she said.

"Gotcha."

Max put the candy in the cart. "You can text me."

"Pardon?"

"Whenever you need me to take you somewhere or do an errand or something. You can send me a text and I'll meet you in the garage. You don't have to come all the way out to come get me."

"Oh. Okay. I'll try to give you a bit of a heads-up. 'Need a ride in about forty-five minutes,' or something. I don't expect you to drop everything at a moment's notice."

"Appreciated." Max hesitated before she asked the next question. "The pick-up we made earlier. Is that going to be a regular thing?"

"I don't know. Why?"

"Because I'd prefer doing it alone without you waiting in the car. Less dangerous for you. Less for me to worry about if something goes sideways."

"Makes sense."

Max carried the bags out to the car, then returned the cart to get her quarter back. Renee watched the transaction like an anthropologist examining a new species.

"All that trouble for a quarter, huh?"

Max shrugged. "It's not about the quarter. It's about keeping the parking lot neat. I don't want my car getting dinged up."

"Not that you'd notice..." Renee said under her breath.

Max didn't say anything.

"I'm not complaining. It adds charm."

"Uh-huh."

They went home so Max could put away her frozen groceries before they thawed. Traffic was light enough that it only took a half hour to get from the crush of downtown to the quiet enclave of Renee's neighborhood. She parked in the garage and turned away Renee's offer to help carry everything inside. The place felt more like a home once she had loaded up the fridge and lined up her cereal and snacks on the counter. Not *her* home, necessarily, but a place where someone might kick off their shoes and relax at the end of the day.

She opened the window and looked out at the pool. The sunlight reflecting off the water made it impossible to see though the glass into the house, but she imagined Renee on the other side going about her business. So she was a driver. She was protection, muscle, intimidation when necessary. She would go into dangerous situations so Renee wouldn't have to.

It was as good a job as any.

Renee went into her bedroom to add what Max had picked up to her stash. There was more than Rand had taken, probably to make up for the inconvenience, so she was better off than she'd been that morning. So technically, she could have a little extra without having it count against her. She wet her lips at the thought, hands flat on the either side of the teapot where she kept the pills. She thought about the dose she had smashed, how good it felt when it slammed into her bloodstream like a wave crashing into her chest. If it was a special treat, she might as well treat herself all the way...

She used the teapot lid to grind three pills into powder, then bent down and took a sharp breath. She straightened and looked at herself in the mirror, smiling as her eyes slid back into focus. She used both hands to push her hair out of her face, tucking it behind her ears. She was calm. She was focused.

Renee walked to her bed and stretched out so she could fully relax. Max was going to be an excellent shield. Protection. Exactly what she needed to stabilize her worst anxiety. It had been a completely ordinary day, but she felt like they'd bonded. A connection had been made. A new world order was in place, and she was excited to see where it would lead.

But first, a nap.

CHAPTER EIGHT

"RENEE LAMAR *shows a quiet grace in the few scenes she's given in* Moon Over Nowhere, *an unnamed wife who nevertheless becomes a living, breathing person in our eyes. Given so little to work with, she creates a character we truly end up caring about."*

The following days were an evolution of their new circumstances. Max, learning to live in someone else's space, and Renee becoming comfortable with a stranger in her bubble. Max got to know Renee's routine, such as it was. Most mornings she went to the gym at six o'clock. She offered to get a membership for Max, who declined because she wasn't comfortable with how much the "fitness center" reminded her of a clone facility from a sci-fi movie. Bright, gleaming, perfect bodies wrapped in as little spandex as possible, humans looking like robots with fake rubber skin stretched over metal frames. It was too creepy for her. She was happy to go back to her normal gym, where she was much more comfortable now that Costello wasn't constantly on her about paying rent.

She got more comfortable in the guest house. She left messes, let the dishes pile up in the sink, draped her dirty laundry over chairs. Small gestures to make it feel like a home instead of a hotel room. A corner of the living room was turned into a home gym, for days when she couldn't make it to Costello's. Usually she ate alone, but occasionally when Renee was home, she would invite Max to eat with her by the pool.

After a week, Renee decided there was no reason for her to accompany Max on every errand. She could pick things up at the store, drop off mail, or deliver contracts just as easily by herself. She wrote up a list of addresses and Max spent an afternoon driving around to make sure she could find each one, and then tried to work up the best route to them so she could save time in the future.

On Friday morning, the hottest day since she'd moved in, and she was trying to work out the intricacies of the air conditioning unit. She was already dressed in a lightweight white T-shirt with the sleeves rolled up, but she was trying to find a different solution before she was forced to strip down any further.

She thought she had the thermostat figured out when she heard a quiet splash from outside. She stepped to the window and peeked out through the blinds. The pool wasn't deep enough for an actual dive, but it seemed as if Renee had stepped off the edge and let herself fall into the water. She was now pushing her hair back against her skull as she moved toward the opposite end of the pool, bobbing in a way that indicated she was stepping on the balls of her feet.

Max shifted her weight, leaning away from the window, but she couldn't quite bring herself to turn her eyes away. She knew she was staring. She knew if Renee spotted her, it would be humiliating at best. Still, she stayed, she ogled.

Renee was in a forest green one-piece, and water dripped off her fingers as she stretched her arms out to either side so she could hang off the pool's edge. She stretched out and let her legs float up to the surface, kicking just a little. She tilted her head back, face to the sun, and her whole body glistened. Max let her attention drift over the exposed bits of Renee's body and admire the way the suit hugged her breasts, how high it was cut on her hips, the paleness of her shoulders and upper chest, both of which were dusted with pale freckles.

"Okay," Max muttered, twisting her head around to focus on something, anything in the living room. The back of her neck burned. She knew that if she stayed, she would be drawn back to the window as long as Renee was in the pool. Simple solution: find something to do in the city. Spend a few hours driving around, then come back when Renee was fully dressed and dry.

She put on her boots and went outside to let Renee know she

was leaving. Renee looked up at the sound of the door opening and let her lower body sink, but she left her arms where they were. Max stopped as far from the pool as she could and pretended to be looking at something on her phone.

"I'm heading out," she said, "if there's anything you need."

"Oh. My dry cleaning should be ready, if you don't mind picking it up." The water splashed as she shifted to point toward the kitchen. "The receipt is magneted to the fridge."

"Great."

Max went into the house to retrieve the receipt. She paused to double-check the address and turned to leave. She stopped mid-step when she saw Renee had lifted herself out of the pool and stood dripping on the stone edge. Her back was to the house and Max was able to see the one part of Renee's anatomy that had been out of view when she was underwater.

"Sweet Jesus," Max muttered. She hoped she wasn't blushing when she walked back outside. She cleared her throat but Renee made no move to cover up. "I might be a while."

"No problem. You're welcome to take advantage."

Max stopped. "Pardon?"

"The pool," Renee said. "Especially on days like today. I don't remember if we covered that. You're more than welcome to take a swim."

"I'll keep that in mind. Have a nice afternoon."

"You too."

Max went back into the guest house to get to the garage. Renee's voice kept ringing in her ears. *You're welcome to take advantage,* with the fact she was practically naked and soaked to the skin made for a very dangerous combination. She didn't need that mental image in her brain. She hoped a little fresh air and distance would help banish it completely. She grabbed her keys and fled, with plans to stay out until darkness fell.

Tattoos. Renee tried not to think about it, tried not to wonder about each and every intricate line, but the word kept circling to the front of her mind from the moment she'd looked up and seen Max standing above her. That alone had been enough to send her mind racing. Max, muscular and dressed in a white shirt and black jeans, looming over her like a deity. But then she saw the tattoos, multiple designs on both arms. They were high enough on her biceps that they would ordinarily be covered even by short sleeves, but today was hot and Max had the sleeves rolled up. Thankfully Max had been distracted by something on her phone so she hadn't seen Renee staring, hadn't seen her lips part with a silent gasp when she saw the ink.

She hoped she was able to keep her voice steady when she spoke, and she was grateful Max had been in such a hurry to leave. She tucked a towel around her chest and went into the house, where took the pitcher of lemonade from the fridge and pressed the chilled glass to her forehead before pouring herself a glass. It had been a while since she had feelings for a woman, long enough that she hesitated to think of herself as bisexual. But she'd known she was attracted to women since she was fourteen. She didn't act on those feelings until she was at a sleepover, when her best friend Samantha asked to share her sleeping bag because it was closest to the space heater.

"This is cozy," Samantha's lips moving against her cheek. Everyone else was asleep, snoring, and they might as well have been in another house entirely.

"Uh-huh," Renee said, stiff and afraid to move an inch. Right now it was just her and Samantha, a warm and soft body lying on the floor next to her.

Samantha cuddled closer. "Roll onto your side. Hold me."

Renee reluctantly did as she was told. They were facing each other now, the first time Renee had been this close to anyone else's face. All she could see were bright eyes, and she could smell minty toothpaste on Samantha's breath. She leaned in and kissed Samantha, changing aim at the last moment so the kiss landed on the corner of her mouth. Samantha giggled and matched the kiss. Renee kissed the other side of Samantha's mouth. Samantha did the same.

Then they kissed.

Samantha made a noise in her throat after a few seconds, and she craned her neck back. "I'm not like that, Renee."

"I know. Me neither. We're just joking, right?"

"...right."

Renee laughed, even as terror swelled in her chest. "Sorry I went too far. I was just kidding around."

"Uh-huh..." She didn't sound convinced, but she also didn't flee the sleeping bag. Renee rolled over, presenting her back so Samantha wouldn't see her wide-eyed terror. After a moment, Samantha spooned her from behind, and they fell asleep like that.

The whole thing seemed forgotten by morning, at least in

Samantha's eyes. It wasn't so easy for Renee to shake. She didn't really know the word bisexual, and it confused her that she couldn't identify herself one way or the other. When she kissed a boy she liked, she felt the same swell of emotion and desire. She figured if she could go either way, she might as well choose the path that was more socially acceptable. Even after she discovered she was bisexual, she maintained the charade. She exclusively dated men, took male dates to red carpet events, pursued men. She turned down roles which would make her play a lesbian, for fear of anyone noticing a tell.

But sometimes… rarely… with someone she trusted…

The first one was Jessica Osbourne, a movie star Renee had admired since she was a teenager. She was older, with just a hint of grey at the temples of her thick black hair. They did a magazine photoshoot together in 2009 with a handful of other women: established stars paired with the faces of the upcoming decade. Jessica was established, and Renee had only appeared in two movies after years of bit roles on TV shows. Jessica took Renee under her wing and made sure the photographer didn't make her do anything too risqué or ridiculous. They had a great time, the pictures looked amazing, and Renee hurried to catch up with Jessica before she left to thank her for the help. They were standing alone by the elevators in the hall outside the studio. Jessica had smiled and said that she was happy to help, that she'd wished for someone to watch over her when she was starting out.

"I also wish there was someone I could have trusted to help me take care of certain needs without worrying it would get out."

Renee had feigned ignorance. "What do you mean?"

Jessica leaned in close to her ear, and Renee had flashbacks to minty toothpaste and the burnt-electric smell of a space heater.

"I mean I saw the way you were looking at me in that photoshoot. You looked like a girl who desperately wanted to get fucked and was also terrified of asking." A hand on her hip, so casual, like punctuation. "Have you ever fucked a woman, little girl?"

Renee somehow managed to say, "No, ma'am."

"But you want to."

"Yes."

It was quiet enough that even Jessica could have barely heard it. But she pressed her lips to Renee's cheek, lifted her hand, and placed something against her palm.

"When you're ready." She stepped back and her voice became more

conversational. She pressed the call button and turned back to Renee, smiling haughtily. "And keep the 'ma'am.' I like that."

The elevator arrived and Jessica stepped into it. She winked at Renee as the doors closed. Renee looked at the card in her hand. It was just a phone number, no identifiers. Renee's hands were shaking so badly she could barely read it, so she slipped it into her wallet. She would get rid of it later. She would shred it, forget she'd ever seen it or heard Jessica say those words.

Three days later, she was knocking on the door of Jessica's penthouse.

Sometimes Renee felt like Jessica was her AA sponsor. They would meet sometimes for coffee and conversation. And some nights, when Renee felt "an urge," she called and went running to wherever Jessica happened to be. There was a definite power dynamic in those encounters. Renee called her ma'am, Miss Osbourne... once "mommy," although that one hadn't gone very far before Renee backed out of it. But it was all play. When Renee broke it off, Jessica wished her well. She even recommended Renee for a role in a period piece that she was doing. She helped get Renee's career off the ground, and she would be forever in her debt for that.

Since then, there had been other trysts. Four women in total, and she hadn't counted how many men. Men were too easy, too quick, for her to count all of them. A date, a quick pass with her hand or mouth, surely that didn't count the same as a full sexual encounter. But she worked hard to ensure those were the only partners the press caught wind of.

She finished her lemonade and looked out at the pool. Tattoos. What was it about those damn tattoos that made her weak? Maybe it was just a sign she needed someone else to slake her thirst. God knew Rand wasn't enough to satisfy her. She'd spent too long on a hamburger when what she really craved was a steak.

Renee was trying to think if there was someone she could call, someone who might come over right away, when her phone rang. She saw Lillian's number and answered.

"Got a call back from Greg, about the Benedict Arnold movie. The nudity *is* non-negotiable, apparently. But I have a feeling they'll cave if we fight a little."

"No, don't bother. I'm sure there's something else I'll want you to fight for by the time we start filming. Save yourself for that."

"Fair enough. You have until April to figure out what you want to ask for."

"And to start a new diet."

She could almost hear Lillian rolling her eyes. "Leave the five pounds on for once. Let the women in the audience see... well, not themselves, because you're still thinner than ninety-nine percent of the population."

Renee laughed. "You get an opinion when it's *your* ass on giant screens all over the world."

"The world doesn't need to count your ribs!"

Renee ended the call with an offer to take Lillian out to lunch so she could confirm she was eating properly. It would have the added benefit of getting her out of the house and away from any thoughts of Max. Lillian arranged to swing by and pick her up in about an hour and poured another glass of lemonade. She took it to the window to look over at the currently-empty guest house. Tattoos. Why was she such a lost cause for tattoos? Why did Max have to have such intriguing ink, hidden until it was far too late to run away and forget they'd ever met? She used her tongue to draw an ice cube into her mouth, pursing her lips around it as it melted and chilled her teeth. She wondered if Max would let her see them up close, examine the details, run her fingers over the design...

She crunched the ice cube, muttered, "Fuck," and dropped the towel as she spun on the ball of her foot to march to the bathroom. She needed to take a cold shower before she met with Lillian.

CHAPTER NINE

"A LIFELESS *adaptation of the cult favorite comic book, Luce Kanon is a blatant attempt to cash in on the superhero boom by people who have no idea what makes those movies appealing. The film is a throwback to the days when superhero movies were a joke, and B-list actors cavorted around in spandex hoping to never be seen outside of a bargain bin. Renee Lamar deserves much better than this bland by-the-numbers embarrassment.*"

Renee's dry-cleaning was under the name Rita Leftbanke, as fake a name as Max could imagine, and one that seemed completely unnecessary. The walls of the shop were covered with autographed headshots of famous customers. But she supposed it was just another example of Renee's paranoia, one more brick in the wall of defense between her and the rest of the world. It was odd how easily she'd adapted to having a near-stranger in her house, but maybe that could be chalked up to how they met. Max came into Renee's life as a protector, a hero.

The pool was empty when she got back to the house. She knocked on the back door before letting herself inside and listening for evidence that anyone was home. She called out and, when no one answered, took the dry cleaning down the hall to leave it in the bedroom. She wasn't entirely sure that was the right option, but it seemed better than just draping it all over the couch and walking away.

The bedroom door was open and she paused on the threshold. It was a lovely bedroom, if a little spartan. A sprawling window seat looked out on the narrow strip of grass that ran alongside the house. It seemed like wasteful, but maybe it was worth it for the amount of sunlight it let in. Everything in the room was neat and tidy and perfectly in place, save for some scattered items on the dresser and a robe which had been discarded on the perfectly made bed.

Max hung the dry cleaning on the dresser and looked back at the robe. She reached out and brushed her fingers over it, testing to see what material it was, and surprised herself by plucking it up and holding it out in front of her. She and Renee probably couldn't wear the same clothes, but the robe was roomy enough that she could get into it with no problem. She told herself to just put it back even as she was sliding one arm into the sleeve, scolding herself as the other arm went in, and sighing with irritation as she straightened the collar.

She went to the floor-length mirror next to the bathroom door. She wondered how many of her outfits she could have bought for the price of this one robe. Probably all the T-shirts she would ever need for the rest of her life. But the material *was* soft against her skin. She imagined how much better it would feel just after the shower, with nothing underneath it. That sent her off on a tangent, the realization that Renee had probably worn this while naked, and she pulled the robe off as quickly as she could without tearing it.

"You're not this girl," she told herself as she put the robe back on the bed. "You don't pine, and you definitely don't pine over mannequins like Renee Lamar."

She came into the living room just as the front door opened, and the woman in question arrived home. She stopped short as if she was a thief who had just been caught breaking and entering. Max also froze, guilty about the fact she'd come so close to being caught in the robe.

Renee ducked her chin and closed the door behind her. "Evening."

"Hey," Max said. "Your dry cleaning is in your room."

"Oh. Thank you. I was out. With a friend."

Max shrugged. "Okay."

"Right," Renee said softly, realizing she didn't have to explain herself.

They stood silently, neither sure how to proceed.

"Who is Rita Leftbanke?"

Renee tilted her head to the side. "What?"

Max said, "Your dry cleaning was under that name. I thought it was weird enough it had to mean something."

"Oh! Oh." She smiled, relaxing a little. "Rita was my grandmother's name. And the Left Banke was a band. They had a big hit in the sixties called 'Walk Away Renee.' My mom loved the song and named me after it. So I thought it was a nice connection and not something people would automatically connect."

Max nodded. "It doesn't really seem necessary. Those pictures on the wall? Even I recognized some of them. You probably don't need to bother with the fake name. I think they'll respect your privacy."

Renee broke her paralysis and crossed into the kitchen. "Yes, well, better safe than sorry."

"Who are you hiding from?"

Renee shook her head, facing the sink instead of looking at Max. "You want to hear about a stalker? Some ex-boyfriend who attacked me one night and turned me into a coward? There's nothing like that. No one has hurt me. In fact, the night we met was the closest I've ever come to even being in a fight. But people jump out at me constantly. Flashing cameras go off in my face when I'm walking to my car. These strangers who know my name come running up to me in public, acting like we're best friends. It's terrifying. So no, I don't have any big trauma. I'd like to keep it that way."

"Fair enough."

Renee kept her back to the room. Max headed out, sensing that she wasn't welcome in the house at this particular moment, but she paused at the door.

"You can text if you need anything tomorrow. I'm free all day."

"Thank you," Renee said quietly.

"You should try to open yourself up more. I'm not one to talk, honestly. But I think it would do you good if you just... I don't know, had a party."

Renee snorted a laugh and finally faced her again. "A party? You must be insane."

Max shrugged. "Nothing huge. Just people you trust."

"That's... I don't think a gathering of that many people would actually count as a party."

"Well. Whatever. I just..." She grimaced and looked down at her feet, regretting the path she'd started down.

"What?" Renee prompted.

"I just think there's a fine line between safe and lonely. That's all."

Renee didn't respond, so Max took the opportunity to escape.

It was dark enough for the pool light to have come on, a pale blue curtain shimmering just below the surface. When she was safely behind the closed door of the guest house, she went to her bed and stripped down to her underwear. Without the bargain-priced shirt and the ripped jeans, she could be any other resident of this insane little neighborhood, one of the people who considered cars to be an impulse purchase. She could have taken some of Renee's dry cleaning, put it on, and walked down the street to see how many of the neighbors she fooled.

"Right," she said, turning away and retrieving her clothes to put them back on. Someone would probably call the cops before she got to the walkway to the beach. Belonging was more than just having the right clothes, and whatever that ineffable quality was, Max knew she didn't have it. She wasn't sure she wanted it.

She held her shirt, rubbing the thin material between her fingers. When it got ripped or otherwise unsuitable to wear, she would just go to Target and buy five more. She didn't want to be the kind of person who needed a designer name no one would see on the tag of her shirt, and she didn't need to shell out her week's grocery budget on a pair of jeans.

After a moment she tossed the shirt onto the bed and went into her bathroom to take a shower, hoping to wash the feeling of Renee's robe off her skin.

In the privacy of her bedroom, Renee opened her teapot and took out two pills. This time she crushed them without thinking or justifying the act, bending down to sniff up the powder as quickly as she used to swallow them. It was such a superior high, so much more bang for each pill, that she doubted she would go back to the original method. The whole act was secret, so what did it matter? She looked at herself in the mirror and brushed the excess dust from her nose, leaning in to make sure her eyes weren't bloodshot.

She tried not to think about the panic stirred by Max's suggestion of a party. She shouldn't be panicking just from the idea of having that many people in her house, but she couldn't deny that it had sent her running for her pharmaceutical security blanket. She took out her phone and began pacing as she thought of who she might call. Rand. No, she didn't want him in the house again so soon after he dipped into her stash. She scrolled through her contacts.

Didn't she have any friends? What happened to that makeup artist from six months ago? She'd been meaning to stay in touch. Certainly they'd exchanged a few texts, but she couldn't find any evidence of it. There had to be someone she considered a friend besides Rand and Lillian. A thin line between safe and lonely, indeed...

She had an idea. She dialed Lillian's number and sat on the foot of her bed, debating the wisdom of her plan even as the line buzzed in her ear. Lillian answered quickly.

"You're practically stalking me today."

"Sorry about that. I just, um, I had a thought. Do you know how many people from the Benedict Arnold cast are in Los Angeles right now?"

She could tell Lillian had switched her to speaker, and now she was writing something down. "Not off the top of my head. Why, what's up?"

"I want to have a party. Like... a bonding thing."

Lillian was silent. "*You* want to have a party? At your house?"

"Yes."

"Like a Christmas party?"

Renee was thrown by that, but she realized it was close to Christmastime. "Yes," she said. "But also a cast get-together. So we can get to know each other before we're stuck together for a few months. Can you make that happen?"

"Well," she could hear the beads clicking in Lillian's mental abacus. "I don't think the entire cast is even locked in yet, not officially. But the biggest hurdle will be parking. Your place doesn't have any. But we can figure something out. When do you want to do this? Say a week before Christmas?"

"That sounds about right. Thank you, Lili."

"Don't thank me until the party starts. I'm going to shuffle some cards and see what happens. I'll call you back in the morning with a better idea of the plausibility. Is there a cap on how many people you want there? Keeping in mind that a couple of the invited guests will see no problem with bringing along a friend or three."

"Try to keep it under thirty."

"I'll see what I can do. What prompted this?"

Renee didn't want to give Max credit for fear of sounding pathetic. "I don't know, call it the Christmas spirit. Plus, it might be nice to meet the people I'm going to be stuck on the wrong coast with while we film this stupid thing."

"Okay. I'm on it. Wish me luck."

"Good luck."

Renee hung up and wrote herself a memo about what she had just done. She didn't always remember things she'd done after taking a pill, so it was nice to have a safety net just in case. She didn't want two dozen actors and actresses swarming into her house a week before Christmas with no memory of why they were there. She also sent an email reminding herself to get food. Parties needed food, and that was the host's responsibility. She put the phone down and leaned forward, elbows on her knees and her face in her hands.

"The hell did you just do," she whispered to herself.

She knew the date now, knew she had just over three weeks to prepare for the invasion she'd just arranged for herself. She hoped it was enough time or, barring that, some cataclysm occurred that would prevent her from having to follow through.

If California was ever going to shake free and fall into the ocean, she suddenly thought Thanksgiving would be a great time for it to happen.

CHAPTER TEN

"QUIET AND *authentic, Past Lives is the sort of movie that seems impossible in an age of billion-dollar blockbusters and deafening spectacle. Renee Lamar imbues the film with a vulnerable, honest portrayal of a woman who has lost everything and considers herself responsible. She's a star in every meaning of the word.*"

California remained stubbornly motionless throughout the end of November, and well into the first week of December. Lillian discovered that seven people from the Benedict cast were in LA, and one more was coming into town for the holiday. She had vocal confirmation from all eight that they would be at the party, and four of them were definitely bringing a date. So twelve people, practical strangers, in her house. That was bad enough, but Renee knew the number would grow before the day arrived. People would find dates, others would invite a friend to tag along...

Then there were the caterers, who were more expensive but much easier to arrange than cooking and serving everything herself. And the valets, who wouldn't actually come into the house but were still part of the mob.

The worst part was when Lillian sent her the guest list and Renee discovered the horrible oversight she'd made in planning the party. She dialed her manager's number before she even closed the email.

"Hello~"

"How many women are in this movie?"

Lillian was thrown for a moment. "Uh. I'm not sure exactly..."

"I should have known. Historical dramas, period pieces, women didn't exist back then unless we were wives or maids." She was pacing now. "I was distracted by the whole thing about being at the forefront of the story."

"There are five female characters in the movie."

"How many have names?"

"Two," Lillian reported, glumly.

Renee scoffed and rolled her eyes. "Unbelievable. Or actually, way too believable."

"It's probably not too late to back out." Lillian quickly added, "Of the party. To back out of the party. Backing out of the movie would be a much bigger headache."

"I know, I know," Renee sighed. She rubbed her forehead. "We'll go ahead with the party. But the next movie I do, I want an all-female cast. Or as close as possible."

"Actually," Lillian said, "I do have a script that isn't filming until late next year. The Benedict movie shouldn't overlap if you're interested in it. Two female leads, and Christina Pinnell is set to direct. It's probably yours for the taking if you're interested."

"Pinnell is great." Renee felt her hope starting to bloom. "What's the elevator pitch?"

"A woman starts an affair with her daughter's teacher, and~"

Renee said, "Wait. It's a lesbian movie?"

Lillian sighed. "Right. Sorry. Instant pass. But are you sure...? It's really not such a big deal..."

"It is for me." She pressed her thumb between her eyebrows. "I'm sorry. I'm not homophobic or anything like that. I would just..."

"I understand, I understand. I'll put it in the 'pass' column and keep looking for something that fits the bill. I'm sorry I didn't warn you the party was trending heavily toward the masculine. At least most of them will probably bring dates, and that will even things up a little. Oh, except for Andrew Kemp. He'll bring his husband. But everyone else..."

"Yeah, yeah. Thanks, Lee."

She hung up and saved the guest list to a notepad on her phone. She would reach out to everyone individually for RSVPs.

She was considering whether she should invite Max through text or in person, and if the invitation would be more than just a courtesy, when her phone rang again. She saw Lillian's face and accepted the call.

"Freddie McCoy!"

"Okay," Renee said.

"Winifred McCoy. I have a note from her on my schedule, and she wants me to find something like what you're trying to find. If the two of you combined forces, if I could let the rumor slip that Freddie McCoy and Renee Lamar were looking to do a project together, the scripts would fly at us. Hell, someone may write something specifically for the two of you. You could have your pick of projects. I can get in touch with her, see if she wants to come to your Christmas party. You can network a little."

Renee knew a lot of McCoy's work. She was good, well-respected in the industry. Social media had a bit of a love-hate relationship with her, but she wasn't going to make a business decision based on some loudmouth idiots with a Twitter account. Lillian was right. A movie with the two of them as headliners was bound to be big news.

"Okay. Yeah, get in touch with her. If she's not available for the party, we can work out a lunch or dinner or something."

"Super!" Lillian sounded thrilled with herself for finding the solution. "Maybe she can bring a couple of friends. Female friends. You could brainstorm your own version of *Ocean's 8*."

"Right now it's just a party invitation," Renee reminded her.

"Absolutely, yes. But it's a Christmas party, and I know what I'm asking Santa for this year."

Renee had been off the phone for about fifteen minutes when Max came in through the garage door. She lifted the bags of groceries as she carried them to the counter.

"The rest is in the car."

"I'll put these away. Thank you." Max nodded and went to get the other bags. She was almost out the door when Renee called to her. "Max? I'm having a Christmas party here in a few days..."

"You want me to clear out?"

"Actually I was going to invite you. If you wanted to come."

Max looked at the floor, shoulders slightly hunched, face unreadable. Renee watched her and assumed she was weighing her options. Finally she shrugged and lifted her chin once, as close to a nod as Renee could expect.

"Okay. Sure." She looked past Renee into the living room. "I'll pick up some decorations. We may need to find someone with a truck to deliver a tree."

"Do you think I need a tree?"

Max shrugged again. "It's your party. But if you want one, it won't fit in my car."

"I'll think about it."

"Okay." She gestured outside. "There's ice cream in the car."

Max disappeared again. Renee looked at the bags and began unloading the groceries.

Renee decided she wanted to go with Max to pick up the decorations. Costello's feelings toward Max had warmed enough that he was more than happy to loan them his truck so they wouldn't have to try loading everything into the backseat of the Plymouth. They went on a Wednesday, both of them assuming the crowds would be more manageable then. He also told her about a home improvement store with a great selection and low prices.

Shopping together was awkward at first but, by the time they started loading up their cart with lights, wreaths, and tinsel, it had become somewhat domestic. Renee also relaxed, transitioning from what Max called turtling - chin down, shoulders up, arms close to her sides, eyes constantly darting around - to a more casual and relaxed posture.

They debated the difference between colored and plain fairy lights, whether they should get a large tree or a smaller one. Max was pro white lights and a small tree, and Renee caved after the weakest of arguments. She admitted it would look nicer and less garish than her choices. But she insisted on getting a wire sculpture of a deer to put on the front lawn.

"So everyone can see the steps up to the house."

Max shrugged and said, "It's your house."

"You don't like it?"

Max looked past her at a light-up meerkat and a nutcracker soldier. "I guess it could be worse."

She tried not to choke at the cash register, where Renee seemed to not even hear the amount as she passed over a credit card. Max again found herself listing the things she could have bought for that amount of money, necessities that would last longer than a single party before being crammed into a closet or a storage room somewhere.

They got back to the truck a little before noon, so Renee suggested grabbing lunch at a nearby restaurant. The problems started as soon as they arrived, waiting at the hostess stand until a table could be cleared. Max noticed a group of three seated in the corner whispering to each other and glancing at Renee. One of them tried to point without lifting her hand, while the man at the table took out his phone to try subtly taking a picture. Renee looked their way once, seemed to acknowledge what was happening, then repositioned herself so her back was to them.

When they had been seated, after giving their drink orders and perusing the menu, Max noticed the man in the corner snapping another photo. Renee ignored it.

"You want me to say something?" Max finally asked. "It *is* what I'm here for."

"They're not hurting anyone. They're just being obnoxious. Can't cause a scene just because someone is being obnoxious."

Max said, "Sure you can."

Renee smiled a little. "Okay. But in this case, it's not worth the hassle. Leave them alone."

Max shrugged and looked out the window.

They ate in peace, with very little conversation beyond the decorations they had just purchased and how best to decorate the house. Max insisted she shouldn't have any input, but Renee insisted. "I need all the help I can get," she said. "I trust you."

"Based on what you saw of my apartment over Costello's? Yeah, I really nailed the Goodwill chic aesthetic."

Renee actually laughed at that.

The gawkers were gone by the time Renee and Max finished their meals. Renee paid and Max followed her from the restaurant, leading her across the street to where they had left the truck. She didn't realize how much distance she'd put between them until she heard someone call out, "Renee! Renee Lamar, just a moment? Just a second?"

She turned back and saw Renee was almost twenty yards behind her, distracted by her phone but looking toward the shouting man as he ran toward her. He seemed to be coming from a small fenced-in lot but, after taking a second to assess the situation, Max decided he must have been crouching next to one of the cars. Lying in wait, as the police report was likely to say. There was another man with him, wearing a flat cap that shaded an unshaven face and big clunky eyeglasses. The man in the lead was brandishing his phone like a sword.

Only two or three seconds had passed since he shouted her name. Renee had turned to face the men fully. She had gone full deer-in-headlights. Max's shoes skittered in the gravel of the parking lot as she changed direction, hoping she was faster than the schlubby guy with the recorder. She assumed he was press or paparazzi, some website journalist who had been tipped off by the peeper inside the restaurant and was now looking for something to keep Twitter occupied through the late afternoon.

"We just want to ask you a few questions about Rand Hurley, Miss Lamar."

Max stepped between Renee and Clickbait. "She doesn't want to talk right now. She's just grabbing some lunch."

Clickbait blinked at Max, as if her existence made him question his worldview. "We're not talking to you, okay? We just want to get a quick~"

"Walk away, or I'll smash your phone."

"Are you threatening me?"

"I'm giving you ample warning of what is going to happen if you persist. Walk away or I'll break your phone. That's the second warning. You won't get a third."

Clickbait was angry now. He stepped forward. "Look, bitch."

Max grabbed his wrist and twisted. He yelped, his fingers twitched, and the phone tumbled to the ground. She only gave it a chance to bounce once before she stomped on it like a cockroach, the screen shattering with a satisfying crackle. Clickbait stared open-mouthed at the wreckage of his phone and slowly lifted his gaze to her, his expression evolving from sad shock to pure rage as he locked onto her.

"You bitch!"

He swung. Max had been hit much harder in the past, even accidental punches had been worse than what he could muster, so she took it without flinching. While he was still in his follow-through, Max returned the punch. She caught him on the ear and sent him flailing backward into his cohort. The flat cap man nearly fell over but managed to keep Clickbait from being completely laid out.

"I can sue you for assault!"

Max advanced on him, kicking the corpse of his phone ahead of her. "If you're going to do that, then I should get my money's worth. That was just a sucker punch. I don't want to waste the police on something like that." She brought up her fists and cracked the knuckles. "Come on, let's make it worth their while, pal."

He bent down to scoop up his phone, never taking his eyes off of her. He put his other hand against the ear she'd punched, checking for blood.

"I just wanted to talk to her!"

"And she just wanted lunch. Neither of you got what you wanted. Walk away now."

Clickbait shoved his crony, and the two men ran away. They only looked back once to make sure she wasn't pursuing. Max remained where she was, checking for rubberneckers but finding the whole scuffle had happened without drawing any attention. She finally allowed the tension to seep out of her shoulders when the men vanished from sight around the corner, and she turned to see Renee staring at her with a wide-eyed, startled expression.

"Sorry," Max muttered. She looked down and opened her hand, brushing at the palm as if she could erase the fact it had just been a fist. "Probably turned that into more than it needed to be."

"No, it's... i-it w-was fine."

Max looked at Renee again. "You okay?"

"Mm-hmm." She swallowed hard and pushed her hair out of her face. She looked back toward the restaurant, then at the truck. "Let's get out of here. Get back home."

"Sure."

They walked back to the truck, heavy silence between them. It had been a good morning, and now Max felt like Renee had withdrawn into her turtle shell, completely locked away again. Maybe that was just how things went in Renee's world. A few carefree hours and then back to the shivering paranoiac. All that money and fame, throwing around hundreds of dollars for a silly party without thinking twice... it was the sort of freedom Max could only dream of.

Renee Lamar might have a charmed life, but it was a hell of a way for a person to live.

CHAPTER ELEVEN

"CHASING GRACE *is a rare rom-com that accepts the uncomfortable parts of falling in love. Partners won't always be perfectly in sync. Love won't always be soaring and all-encompassing. Acknowledging ugly truths without letting them weigh down the romance heightens the charm and makes the courtship of Renee Lamar and Kyle Seabrook all the more believable.*"

The day of the party, Max accepted delivery for what Renee called "the only decoration that matters": a case of booze. The guest list had grown to about twenty people, and Renee was taking a nap to prepare herself for the onslaught. She also didn't like accepting her own deliveries for fear of how easily someone could spread the word that they knew where a real movie star lived. Max went back and forth between thinking Renee was overly sensitive and thinking the measures were justified. God knew there were stalkers, and other jerks like Clickbait running around looking for the perfect candid shot, maybe overkill was better than crossing her fingers and hoping people would respect her privacy.

The living room had been transformed into a spectacular Yule explosion. Silver and gold tinsel were strung around the room, and the lights around the windows would be set to twinkling as soon as the sun set. The smaller tree was definitely the correct choice. It was unmissable, but also didn't take up too much room. The house wasn't small, but any room would be cramped with almost two dozen people in it.

Renee woke up when the caterers arrived and warily watched them set up in her kitchen. She had changed into a white button-down with billowing sleeves and black slacks. The shirt was long enough that it draped almost to her knees. Max didn't have an artistic eye, but the red of Renee's hair was striking against the sharp whiteness of the blouse, and the two colors combined to make her skin look flushed and pink. It was a very good look for her.

Max was in a black vest over a white V-neck and her nicest pair of black jeans. It was the closest she got to actually dressing up, although she did get her hair done out of deference to Renee's reputation. She thought she looked ridiculous, but she knew she would be glad she'd done it when the Hollywood egos started showing up in their finery.

She was in the kitchen when the first guest arrived. He was someone she didn't recognize, naturally, but he carried himself like someone who expected to be Known in any room he entered. Renee introduced him as Henry Bishop. He was tall, broad-shouldered, built like he'd played football in college and kept up his physique even though he hung up his pads fifteen years ago. Max idly wondered who a black man would be playing in a movie set in the American Revolution, but maybe they were doing the Hamilton thing with color-blind casting.

After Bishop came a whippet-thin man with a weasel face but a gorgeous smile. He actually took the time to detour into the kitchen to say hello to the catering staff, which earned him points in Max's book. Bishop and his wife were dressed in matching red sweaters like they were heading to a Christmas card photo shoot after the party, but this man - identified as Robert Nelson - wore a tailored black suit.

People started arriving in clusters, more people than Renee could identify and Max knew she would never retain their names even if she'd tried. She heard names - George, J. Alton, Michael - but never managed to link faces to them.

Renee made a point of introducing Max to a statuesque brunette with a husky voice and sleepy eyes. "This is Lillian," Renee said, "she's the one who finds all my work."

"The work comes to her these days," Lillian said, taking Max's hand for a quick squeeze. "I just try to figure out the right ones to offer her."

There was a bit of a fuss when Olivia Childress, the only other actress in the movie playing a named character, arrived with her plus-one. Judging from the reactions, the raven-haired woman was also a celebrity of some sort. She was certainly gorgeous enough to be famous. Max was in the dark until friendly-if-weaselish Robert Nelson took pity on her.

"Lana Kent," he said, leaning close so only she would hear. "Lead singer of Radiation Canary. They're a solid band. You've probably heard some of their stuff without realizing it."

"Possible," Max admitted.

It was a half-hour later, with the party in full swing, when Max found herself at the punch bowl with the singer. Lana smiled politely and Max offered a head-nod.

"I have a rude question," Lana said.

"Okay."

"Should I know who you are? I only ask because I can tell you're not staff, and you don't seem to be here with anyone."

Max smiled. "No. I'm no one. I'm... fame-adjacent, I guess."

Lana nodded and refilled her punch. "That's fine. I was just curious. I only badgered Olivia into bringing me along because my partner loves Renee Lamar. I'm trying to get up the courage to ask for an autograph."

"I can make that happen for you."

"Really? I don't want to impose..."

Max shrugged. "It'll give me purpose." She scanned the room until she saw Renee by the tree and stepped away from the table. "Come on."

Lana hesitated long enough to create a gap between them, but eventually she followed. Renee saw them coming and turned to face them, raising her eyebrows and tilting her head to the side.

"Renee. Have you met Lana?"

"I haven't had the pleasure," Renee said, offering her hand. "I'm a very big fan. We used to listen to *Action After Warnings* in the makeup trailer on *Dark Horse*."

Lana grinned. "Wow. That's amazing. I loved that movie. I can't believe our music was on set." She blinked and seemed to lose her train of thought. "Uh. Uh, Avery. My partner. She owns all your movies. Two copies of some of them. It would mean the world to her if I could maybe get an autograph..."

"I'll do you one better than that. It's Christmas, right? I'm sure

I have something around here I stole from a movie set. I'll find something good and sign it for her. And I'll give her a call and say hello."

Lana looked stunned. "Wow. That would be amazing. I would owe you…" She smiled. "I would owe you a song."

"I couldn't ask you to work at a party."

"A party I crashed for selfish purposes. It would make us even."

Renee drained her cup and put it down, gesturing for Lana to follow her. "Come on. I'll see what swag I have. We'll see if I can find you a guitar, too."

Both women seemed to have forgotten Max was there, which was fine by her. She was amazed by the transformation in Renee. Any anxiety she had was gone. So far she'd been the consummate hostess, moving through the crowd, laughing and chatting with everyone for an appropriate amount of time before moving on. The fear and tension which had been leading up to the party was nowhere to be seen, and Max was relieved to see the idea seemed to have worked out.

She, on the other hand, was getting a little sick of the constant glances from celebrities, the questions asked under the breath, the general "who is this strange person in Renee's house" aura she got whenever any of the celebrities looked at her.

Confident that Lana would keep Renee occupied, Max refilled her glass and headed out to get some fresh air by the pool. The lights were on under the water but the yard was otherwise dark, and there was just enough of a nip in the air to make her wish she'd worn long sleeves. She tilted her head back and looked up at the smoggy aurora swirling above the city.

"I can't think of a way to let you know I'm here without spooking you."

Max didn't jump. She pivoted her head slowly toward the voice, which belonged to a woman stretched out on the pool chair, which was angled in a way to make her invisible from the house. She wore a white suit, which seemed to glow in the dim light. Her hair was short, black, and styled up in a pompadour. Her bare feet were crossed at the ankle, and she held an empty glass of champagne on one knee. Her high heels were artfully discarded on the deck next to her. She looked like she belonged on an album cover.

"I can go back in if you want to be alone," Max said.

"No, don't do that. There's far too many people in there." She ran her eyes down the length of Max's body and then slowly back up to her face. "You don't look like you fit into that crowd anyway."

"I'll take that as a compliment."

The woman smiled. "Do. I love wallflowers. I collect them and make beautiful bouquets." She brought her glass to her lips, which twisted in disappointment when she discovered it was empty. Max stepped closer and offered her glass. "Ah, my savior. Thank you, darling."

"Max."

"Freddie McCoy. So what do you do, Max?"

"Errands."

"Hm. Mysterious."

Max shrugged. "Boring."

Freddie took a sip of her drink and uncrossed her legs, unfolding herself from the chair with a grace Max wouldn't have thought possible. When she stood, she was a few inches taller than Max even without her heels. She had a hint of an accent that was too subtle to pinpoint, but it made her clip the end of certain words.

"You don't seem boring to me, Max." She brought her hand up and let two fingers lightly brush the line of Max's jaw. "You look like you've led a very interesting life."

Max tensed, only relaxing when Freddie's hand fell back to her side. "We all have a past."

"I bet it's a fascinating story. Maybe we should continue this discussion inside."

"I thought you said there were too many people in there."

Freddie nodded over Max's shoulder. "I actually meant in there."

Max turned to see she had indicated the dark guest house. Freddie's voice had dropped low until it was almost a purr, and it felt like each word was an invisible finger running up the back of her neck. Max was terrible at knowing when women were flirting with her. Even when she was fairly sure, the small percentage of doubt always kept her from making a move. Tonight, though, she felt confident enough to take a shot. She faced forward again and tried to read the message behind Freddie's eyes.

"I don't think we should go in there."

"And why not?"

"Because if we go in there, I'm going to fuck you."

Freddie raised an eyebrow, her lips curling into a slow smile.

"Well." She drained her glass, bent her knees so she could place it on the deck, and then straightened like a cobra emerging from a charmer's basket. She held Max's gaze without speaking before she stepped around her and walked to the guest house. Max remained where she was for a beat, then turned to follow.

Freddie stopped at the door and waited for Max to open it for her. Max stepped backward into the house and let Freddie follow her, but she grabbed Freddie's hand to keep her from venturing farther inside. She shut the door with a flip of her fingers and used her other hand to push Freddie against it, covering her new friend's body with her own. Freddie allowed herself to be kissed, oddly passive beyond wrapping her arms around Max's waist.

"Are you just going to let me take charge?" Max asked when the kiss ended.

"You seemed to have a pretty firm idea of how this would go."

"Oh, I do."

"Pray tell."

Max stepped closer, their hips pressing together, and kissed her again, thrusting with her tongue and moaning as Freddie responded in kind. She broke the kiss and moved her lips close to Freddie's ear. "First I'm going to take off your clothes," she said as her hands moved between them, fingers deftly working the buttons of Freddie's suit jacket. "I know your lips taste like champagne, but I'm going to find out what the rest of you tastes like. Your tits. Your stomach. Your thighs. Your pussy."

She licked Freddie's cheek, shifting her thigh forward. Freddie straddled it and squeezed.

"More," Freddie said.

The suit jacket was undone, so Max started on the buttons of her shirt. "I don't normally talk this much."

"But when the reward is this sweet..."

Max had to admit, the woman had a point. She slid her hands under the shirt. "I'm going to take you over to the couch, throw you down on the cushions, run my tongue over your whole body..."

Freddie shivered and raked her fingers over Max's back. "Yes."

"I'm going to put your legs on my shoulders and let you hold me down." Her hand moved lower and discovered Freddie was wearing a belt. She fumbled with it, and Freddie moved one hand to help her get it undone. "I'm going to make you wet," Max promised, "drive you crazy. But I'm not going to let you come."

"No...?"

"Not with my mouth. You're going to tell me when you're going to come. And I'm going to move back up your body. I'm going to put my hand against you... like this..."

Freddie grunted, the tail end of the sound tapering off into a moan.

"And you're going to ride me until you come on my hand. And then~"

"Max..." Breathless.

"Yeah..."

"Shut up and get to work."

Max grinned and, leaving her hand where it was, pulled Freddie to the couch.

CHAPTER TWELVE

"WHITE BLUFFS *only truly comes to life in the later scenes, when Renee Lamar arrives on the scene as a park ranger tasked with saving our inept protagonists. There's a much better movie to be found by following her character and leaving most of the morons fumbling on the mountain off-screen, but unfortunately the movie had little interest in that.*"

Renee tapped her fork against the side of her glass to get everyone's attention. She'd found a guitar and Lana deemed it to be suitable for their needs. Those at the party who recognized Lana brightened when they saw her carrying the instrument, and Renee smiled wide as they gathered closer. There was nothing in the house that could approximate a stage, but the sunken living room created the impression that Lana was on a platform. Renee pulled over a stool from the kitchen counter so Lana could sit with the guitar on her lap.

"Everyone, hi, uh, we have a special treat tonight. Some of you know Lana Kent from her band Radiation Canary. She and I worked out a, uh, barter exchange which means I can put her to work for a little bit at the party."

"I still think I'm getting the better end of the deal," Lana said. "I'm happy to do a few songs."

Gordon Helms, the man who would play Benedict Arnold,

said, "Are you going to play something new for us?"

Lana said, "I was planning to do some Christmas songs, but sure. I have a new one I can debut. It won't be the same without the rest of the band, but I'll do my best."

She began to play, and Renee moved off to the side so she wouldn't steal the symbolic spotlight.

"I've never heard a song with your name in it," Lana sang, "So I don't have an excuse for why I'm saying it. Can't explain why it's always on the tip of my tongue. Because no one's ever put your name into their song..."

Renee scanned the crowd. It was a good party. People were enjoying themselves, bonding, laughing. Now they were focused on a famous singer who was performing a new song. And it was all thanks to her. She kept waiting for panic to set in, either about something going wrong or anxiety about having so many strangers in her house, but she was calm. She hadn't told anyone, not even Lillian, but she'd taken two Xanax before lunch. She knew it was bad to mix Xanax with her oxy, but as long as she didn't take them both in the same day, it should be fine.

And it felt fine. She felt at peace for the first time in ages. She might have to find a schedule that would let her use both pills, something safe and balanced.

"There's no excuse for why your name is stuck in my head," Lana sang, "No innocent reason it was what I accidentally said..."

Renee scanned the room for Max and realized she hadn't seen her in quite a while. She looked over her shoulder, out the windows onto the patio, and saw a champagne glass standing next to the pool. Had she run away to the safety of the guest house? She hoped Max hadn't felt overwhelmed by the party. It wasn't that so many of the guests were famous; she got the feeling Max wouldn't recognize Tom Hanks if he walked in wearing a name tag. But a whole house full of people she didn't know would still be a lot to deal with. Max and crowds didn't go well together.

Lana finished the song and transitioned into "Have Yourself a Merry Little Christmas" as the guests applauded. Renee took the chance to step away, slipping through the back door and crossing the patio. She would just offer a quick apology, a thank-you for everything Max had done to make the party happen, and wish her a good night. A year-end bonus would probably be a nice gesture, too.

The guest house was dark, and Renee wondered if Max had already gone to bed. She stepped off the grass and cupped her hand to peek in the window to see if she could see any lights on in the bedroom.

Max was on the couch, vest unbuttoned and T-shirt pushed up to reveal bared breasts. She was perched on top of someone, one hand braced on the back of the couch, the other between her and whoever was writhing on the couch beneath her. Renee could see bare shoulders and long slender legs hooked on Max's hips, but there was no way to identify who it was until she saw the white suit jacket pooled on the floor.

Freddie.

At the moment she made that realization, Max lifted her head slightly and looked directly at her. Her face was red from exertion, a vein pulsed from her eyebrow to hairline, and even in the dim light, a sheen of sweat was shining on her throat.

Renee froze. Max's lips curled into a smile and her arm flexed. She thrust her hips forward, and Freddie arched up to meet her. Freddie cupped Max's breasts, her thumbs pinching and twisting the nipples, and now that Renee was watching them she could hear faint sounds through the glass: Max grunted and bent down for a kiss, which stifled Freddie's moan as Max did something between her legs.

Freddie put one hand on Max's shoulder and pulled herself up, kissing her neck. Max lifted her eyes to the window again. If she was surprised to see Renee still standing there, it didn't register in her admittedly glazed eyes. She moved her hand from the back of the couch to the back of Freddie's head, digging her fingers into the hair with what looked like a violent grip.

Renee shifted her weight onto the outside of her foot, leaning away from the house in an attempt to walk away. But she didn't follow through. She just stood there awkwardly and watched Max pull Freddie's head back and kiss her hard. Their bodies moved in concert, arch meeting thrust and combining into a fluid motion of two bodies. It was beautiful. And Max had seen her watching and made no attempt to stop or cover up, so was that tacit permission to keep watching? Even if Freddie hadn't consented?

Max was looking at her again. Her eyes were dark, as if the pupils had swelled to completely overtake the whites. She lifted two fingers and made a curling motion. Renee flinched. Was it a 'come inside' move? No. No, this was horizontal, this was...

Touch yourself.

Renee swallowed the lump in her throat. The night was chilly, but sweat had broken out on her brow. Her mouth felt impossibly dry. But she put one hand against the adobe wall, and she pressed the other against the crotch of her slacks. She could hear Lana Kent singing faintly from the house. She had transitioned into a duet of "Fairytale of New York" with Andy Kemp. What she was doing was scandalous and wrong, and if anyone at the party came out and caught her, she would be mortified. She would have to drop out of the movie, she would have to take a hiatus...

Max sat up again and shrugged out of her vest, then took off the T-shirt and tossed it aside. She stayed upright, Freddie's legs wrapped around her waist, Max's hand still cupping her, but Renee's focus was higher. She could only stare at the sculpted and inked muscles of Max's shoulders, biceps that bulged with every movement, small breasts bared to reveal small dark nipples that were wet from attention from Freddie's lips and tongue.

And the tattoos, now on full display. They formed a shoulder holster of ink across her collarbones, almost bat-like in shape, the wings stretching down her upper arms.

Renee choked back a gasp, but she parted her legs and pressed her fingers to the crotch of her pants, pushing hard and rubbing the material against her now-sensitive skin.

Freddie put her hands on Max's chest and raked her fingernails down. She followed the curve of Max's breasts, down her ribs, and splayed her fingers across Max's tight stomach, framing the pucker of her navel before moving outward to hold her hips. Freddie's lower body was off the cushion now, and she cried out loud enough that Renee was worried it might be heard in the party even though everyone had now joined in on the chorus of the Pogues' song.

Max pulled Freddie up to her and they kissed again. Freddie put her hands on Max's shoulders and pushed with her lower body, repositioning them until Max was on her back with her head against the opposite arm of the couch. Freddie began kissing her way down Max's body, taking a slow and methodical route. Max let one foot fall onto the floor, spreading her legs in anticipation of Freddie's destination. She played with Freddie's hair with one hand putting the other behind her own head in the casual, relaxed posture of someone who knew she was about to get laid.

And her eyes were locked on Renee, who was now moving her hips against her hand. Her other hand had curled into a fist against the wall, and she knew her breathing was ragged. She was grunting quietly and prayed it couldn't be heard through the window, dreaded the idea of Freddie turning around and seeing her.

The music stopped, and Renee heard a murmur of voices amid the applause. It was enough to break her hypnosis, and she finally retreated. She stooped to pick up the champagne glass and drained what little was left as she went back into the house. She hoped she wasn't flushed or sweating, but everyone seemed too focused on Lana to pay close attention to her. She went into the kitchen, filled the glass with water, and emptied it in one swallow.

Was this glass Max's or Freddie's? she wondered, *What are the lips that touched this glass touching right now?*

That thought required another full glass of water. The buzz of arousal and her aborted masturbation session had combined with coming down off the Xanax to make her feel like she was about to erupt and hit the ceiling. She was still drinking the second glass when she became aware of someone standing next to her. She turned to see Lana holding the guitar, and she managed a smile.

"I'm going to have to find something really good for your partner," Renee said. "No one expected you to do a whole mini-concert."

"It's my fault," Lana said. "Once I get going, it's tough to stop."

Renee offered a weak smile and put the glass down next to the sink. "Come on. Let's go see if I can find a costume shirt for you to take home. I've stolen quite a bit of stuff from pretty much everything I've done. Does she have a favorite movie of mine?"

She ended up finding a blouse from her latest movie, *Never Lost Nobody*, signed a poster for the same movie, and made a call to wish Lana's partner a merry Christmas. By the time she'd fulfilled all her promises, the guests were starting to migrate toward the door. Renee distracted herself with the goodbyes, telling her soon-to-be costars that she couldn't wait to work with them. Gordon Helms said he was looking forward to being married to her, and she was too distracted to be irritated by the comment.

Renee's emotions had almost stabilized when Freddie came strutting in from outside. She somehow managed to look completely fresh and polished, her suit immaculate and every hair in place. She spotted Renee and crossed the room directly to her. Renee tried to think of a way to escape but she couldn't manage it without drawing attention to herself. The room had mostly cleared out and she had no one nearby she could use as a lifeline.

Freddie said, "Renee. I'm very disappointed we didn't get a chance to talk tonight. That seems to be the way these industry parties go, I'm afraid."

"Mm-hmm," Renee said. "Yeah, we'll... we just couldn't seem to find a moment to sit down and talk. But I hope we can reschedule."

"Absolutely." She was already taking a billfold from her jacket pocket - Renee could only see how the sleeves had sprawled on the floor of the guest room - and withdrew a card. "Give me a call any time this week. I generally don't schedule meetings this close to Christmas, so I'll be free for lunch whenever you are."

Renee took the card. "Great. Thanks, that's... I'm free, too. So we'll find a time that works for us both."

"Fantastic." She closed the billfold and concealed it back in her jacket. Then, as casually as the rest of the conversation, she said, "I know what you saw. Max told me."

Renee went still. "Oh."

Freddie grinned. "You really know how to throw a fantastic party, Renee. Can't wait to see what happens on New Year's." She winked and turned away, leaving Renee in a stunned stupor.

The rest of the crowd left in short order, and the caterers went not long after. Renee could almost feel the silence flooding back into the room like a physical essence. She closed the door, locked it, and leaned against it with a sigh of relief.

Then Max came into the room.

They were separated by the expanse of the living room and kitchen, basically the entire width of the house acting as a buffer, but Renee still felt crowded. Max had put her vest back on, but not the T-shirt. Her chest and arms were exposed, the tattoos on almost full display. Renee tried to wet her lips, but all the moisture had evaporated from her mouth.

"Everyone gone?"

"Yeah."

"You missed the end of the show."

Renee blushed. "Well. I... I had... the party was..." She tucked her hair behind her ears and went to the kitchen just so she wasn't standing awkwardly by the door.

"Right," Max said under her breath. She had her hands in her pockets, arms tight to her sides. She looked down at the floor and shifted her weight from the front of her feet to the heels, like someone waiting for a bus. "I'm not sure what's appropriate here after that."

"Neither am I." Renee filled another glass with water and

drained it. "It happened. I think we both, um, we both *appreciated* what was happening."

"All three of us did," Max said.

Renee nodded. "But I don't think it's something that should be repeated."

Max said, "Okay."

"You're fine with that?"

Max shrugged. "It's not like I arranged for it to happen. It was fun. But if you think it should be a one-time thing, I have no problem with that."

Renee nodded. "Okay then."

"You need help cleaning up?"

Renee hadn't even had time to think about that. She looked at the mess, the napkins and paper plates and forgotten cups littering her home.

"Yes. But tomorrow."

"Okay. See you then."

Renee didn't hear her leave but, when she looked back, the room was empty. She sighed heavily and turned off the overhead light, stepping out of her shoes and leaving them where they were as she went down the hall to her bedroom. She shed her party clothes as soon as she was through the door and went to the dresser in her underwear. She stared down at the teapot. She was horny, frustrated, and on the verge of a crash. Taking oxy and Xanax in the same day was bad. But it was late in the day. The Xanax had to be almost out of her system. It certainly felt like it was gone.

She took out one pill - just one single pill to stabilize things until she could fall asleep - and crushed it with the teapot lid. The resulting powder was so sparse she thought it was likely she'd inhaled more dust than anything else, but she wouldn't take another. She sniffed and brushed at her nose, turning on one foot and walking to her bed.

She would just lie down, rest her eyes, and finish getting undressed in a few minutes. For now she just needed her mood to settle, and to let the energy of the party seep out of her bones. She smoothed her hands over the blanket and marveled at how cool it felt against her cheek as she fell asleep.

CHAPTER THIRTEEN

"DON'T LOSE *Your Head! Sources say Renee Lamar is indeed returning to the hellish Zarins Asylum for* BEDLAM II: DOOR TO MADNESS, *which will be odd for fans who remember her character's gruesome and shocking end in the first movie.*"

The sun had just topped the wall at the edge of Renee's property when Max came out of the guest room the next morning. She hadn't slept long, or very well, but she'd avoided alcohol well enough that she wasn't hungover. When she got into bed the night before, she'd used her phone to do a quick search for Freddie McCoy just to see how famous she was. The answer seemed to be 'quite a bit.' She had a long list of credits stretching back to the early aughts, and for the first time, she wished she had Netflix or one of those other services that let you watch movies without paying for each one.

Google provided a trio of YouTube videos of her appearances on talk shows. She clicked on one at random and saw a column of related videos on one side of the page. One of them was titled "Freddie McCoy's Top Sexy Moments." She clicked on that, which turned out to be a montage of scenes: Freddie dry-humping a man in what looked to be a cellar, being frisked by a woman in leather, sitting in a hot tub, striding across a windswept roof in a ballgown that whipped around her legs like a dervish.

Her hair was almost always longer than it had been at the party, which Max found disappointing. The pompadour suited Freddie very well, and she hoped it was a new look rather than something she'd done for a role.

She ended up watching videos for almost two hours before her phone's battery finally died. She'd slept well, with lots of amazing dreams, but now it was time for her to earn her keep.

The house wasn't in the shambles she would have expected. She thought Hollywood celebrities would think nothing of leaving a mess, walking away and letting "the help" deal with it. But it seemed they were very careful to be tidy, or maybe just one enterprising guest had taken it upon themselves to gather as much of the empty cups and plates as possible.

It didn't even take Max a full half hour to get everything into a trash bag, which she took out to the bin in the garage. A guitar was sitting on the divan. She assumed it was kept in the bedroom, since she'd never seen it anywhere else in the house and there wasn't room for it in the front closet. She took the instrument by the neck and carried it down the hall. She knocked on the bedroom door, waited for a response, and let herself in.

Renee was sprawled on top of the blankets in her underwear, legs slightly spread with her feet hanging off the edge of the mattress. Her arms were curled up protectively around her head. Max almost tripped over her feet and retreated.

"Shit, sorry... I'm..." She paused and pushed the door open again, watching for any signs of life from the bed. "Renee?" The feet didn't even twitch, so she rapped loudly on the door. "*Renee.*"

Max put down the guitar and crossed the room in two steps. She climbed onto the bed, jostling Renee and pushing her onto her side. Renee's arms flopped limply, but she released a quiet choked groan of protest as she was repositioned. Max checked her pulse - slow and erratic - and pushed open Renee's eyelids to check the pupils. Her skin was clammy. Max straightened and looked around the room until she spotted the little teapot sitting on the dresser. She lightly patted Renee's cheek.

"Renee, what did you take? Can you tell me that?" She pressed her knuckles against Renee's sternum and pressed hard, rubbing back and forth.

Renee grunted and brought her hands up, pushing blindly at Max's forearms. "Stop that... don't..."

"Are you okay? Renee, are you awake? I need you to look at me."

"M'so tired..."

"Tough shit. Wake up."

Renee opened her eyes and looked up at Max, blinked, and then her entire upper body convulsed. Max anticipated what was about to happen and pushed Renee back onto her side. She moved out of the way before Renee threw up. The blanket was probably ruined, but Max had been spared the vast majority of damage. Renee heaved again and came up empty, and she put her hand over her mouth with a sob. Max rubbed her shoulder.

"You okay?"

"Dunno..."

"Okay," Max said. "I'm going to go get a phone so I can call 911. I'll be~"

Renee slapped her arm, then grabbed a handful of her shirt. "No. Oh god, you c-can't."

"You~"

"We don't do that, okay?"

Max didn't know if 'we' was in reference to the two of them, or if she meant celebrities in general. Either way, she didn't have many options.

"Fine. Is there someone who can check you out, make sure you're okay?"

Renee nodded, forcing herself to swallow. "I didn't overdose. Not a real overdose. I just... mixed pills. Stupid." She flopped back onto the bed, angled away from the mess she'd made, and put one hand over her eyes.

"Don't tell anyone," she said.

"I signed the paper," Max said. "Where's your phone?"

Renee pointed to the dresser and Max went to get it, but the phone was nowhere to be seen. She did see the remnants of powder on the wood, and the teapot was still open to reveal a little baggie full of little round pills. It was obvious what had happened from the moment she saw Renee on the bed, but she was still shaken by the physical evidence of the part she'd played in the situation. If she hadn't picked up these pills...

No time for that now. She looked around and saw Renee's slacks on the floor. She retrieved them and found the phone in the back pocket. She took it back to the bed, where Renee had managed to sit up. Her legs were folded in front of her, and she was hunched forward with her head over her lap.

"Are you going to throw up again?"

She shook her head. She brought her hand up and pressed it against one eye. Max waited until she looked up before offering the phone.

"I can put your blanket in the laundry."

"That's not part of your job."

Max said, "It's close enough. Come on, get up. Go in the bathroom and get washed up. Splash some cold water on your face, at least."

"Thank you."

She got up and Max gathered the blanket, folding it around the mess. When she carried it out of the room, Renee turned and zombie-walked into the bathroom. The sound of running water followed Max down the hall. She took the blanket into the laundry room and did her best to clean it up. She'd seen far worse in the locker rooms and bathrooms at Costello's. As long as there wasn't any blood, she could handle anything. She hated blood.

Renee was in the living room when Max came back into the house. She had put on a pair of faded and torn jeans and a T-shirt with a collar that had been stretched into an unnatural shape. Her hair was wet and she wasn't wearing makeup. The radiant shine of her skin was probably sweat from throwing up, but Max had to admit she didn't look bad.

"So," Max said. "Does that sort of thing happen often?"

"No. Never. Last night was a unique case."

Max said, "Because of the party, or because of what happened at the party?"

Renee smiled and lowered herself gingerly onto the couch. "It's not your fault."

"I got the pills for you."

"Right," Renee said softly. Her hair had fallen into her face and she tossed her head, not bothering to do anything to actually solve the problem. "I would have gotten them anyway. And... and speaking of..." She flexed her toes and avoided Max's gaze. "I-I'm running a little low..."

"Do you want more," Max asked, "or do you *need* more?"

Renee glared at her. Max held the stare until Renee looked away.

"Fine, if I can't take the blame for that, I still talked you into throwing the party. And then I put on a special show for you in the backyard. So if last night pushed you over some kind of edge..."

Renee was shaking her head slowly. "The only part you can take credit for is being here to wake me up. I knew the risks of that shit. I could have gone into a coma. I don't think one pill would have done anything that drastic, but..." Her voice faded to a whisper. "I don't know... I don't know what might have happened, but I'm glad you were there."

Max shuffled her feet awkwardly.

"The doctor is on the way. He's discreet. If you called 911, it would be trending on Twitter within the hour and I have a press tour coming up. It would be the top question from every idiot with a movie website or YouTube channel. So thank you for sparing me from that."

Max had flashbacks to Miriam Rudd, the fight that ended her career, another woman in her orbit who had slipped into a coma and never woke up. She found herself suddenly overwhelmed with a low-level panic of what might have happened - *Wrecker Reszke Found Standing Over Another Dead Woman* - and flinched as if she could actually hear the words being read on television.

"I'll leave you alone for the doctor--"

"Don't," Renee said. "I don't want to be alone right now."

Max hesitated but then came into the living room. She sat on a chair facing Renee, her hands resting on her knees. She didn't know where to look. Renee seemed to be trying to fold in on herself and become invisible, so Max turned her head and looked out the window. The ocean was vibrant and blue even with a haze of fog obscuring the horizon line.

She sat silently and watched it, waiting to see if it would dissipate before the doctor arrived.

Max went outside when the doctor arrived so she could give Renee some privacy. The ocean was much more of a spectacle without the window in the way. Feeling the breeze off the water, smelling it even this far away, reminded her of just how vast it really was. She was sitting on the front steps when a car screeched to a stop in the driveway and the tall brunette she'd met the night before jumped out and stormed the house like a coach coming to scold a losing team. It took her a moment to remember the woman's name was Lillian. Today her eyes weren't sleepy. They were wide and filled with fury.

"Where is she?" Lillian demanded as she ascended the stairs.

Max stood up. "Inside. With the doctor." Lillian started to step around her, but Max blocked her. "With the doctor," she repeated.

"Listen, you little pissant..."

Max put her hand on Lillian's shoulder. She only applied enough pressure to make it clear she could apply much more.

"She's with the doctor. Likely having a private conversation. You can go in when they're done."

"Renee *called* me and told me to come over."

"She hired me to protect her. That's all I'm doing."

Lillian snorted. "You're doing a bang-up job." She put her hands on her hips and paced, moving off the stone steps into the grass. She looked at the ocean and then spun on Max, aiming a finger at her. "Do you think I don't know who you are? I looked you up. As soon as Renee told me she was hiring someone, and they were living in her house, I found out everything I could about you. Maxine 'Wrecker' Reszke. Does she know? Have you told Renee about your claim to fame?"

Max took a breath and let it out slowly. "She doesn't need to know."

"That you're a murderer?"

"I'm not a..." Max took another breath. "We both signed waivers before the match. We stayed within the rules. It was a clean fight."

Lillian rolled her eyes. "That makes it all better."

"It makes it legal," Max said. "Nothing makes it better."

There was a glimmer of compassion in Lillian's eyes. She looked away without saying anything.

"You obviously know Renee pretty well," Max said. "If I treated her like a little kid, if I flushed her pills and scolded her about mixing them, how do you think she would react?"

"Dig her heels in and kick you out," Lillian grumbled.

"I protect her to the best of my ability. That doesn't include slapping pills out of her hand. But it does cover stopping people from barging in on her private moments"

Lillian huffed but dropped her hands from her hips. "Fine," she said in a small, defeated voice.

Max didn't let down her guard in case Lillian tried to rush the house. She crossed her arms over her chest and waited as Lillian paced, head bowed to look at her phone.

The door finally opened, and the doctor emerged. Lillian took two quick steps toward the house, but Max stopped her with a look.

Lillian made a face, but she stopped where she stood. Max nodded her thanks, then did the same to the doctor, and went to the threshold of the house to look inside. Renee was sitting at the kitchen counter with her back to the door, one hand curled into a fist next to her head. She seemed to be staring into a tall glass of water.

"Lillian is here. Do you want to see her?"

"No." Renee sounded like she was crying. "But she can come in anyway."

Max motioned Lillian to come in. She stepped out of the way before she could be steamrolled.

"Was it on purpose?" Lillian demanded as soon as she was inside.

"No!" Renee shouted back. "God, of course it wasn't."

"Well, it was either a stupid choice or a stupid accident. It's good to know what we're dealing with."

Renee looked back and saw Max lingering by the door. "You can come in too, if you want."

"I think I'll let you two sort it out. I can go make that pickup you mentioned."

"Are you sure?"

Max shrugged. "I'm here for whatever you need, Renee."

"Thank you."

"Sure. I have some cash, you can repay me."

Renee nodded and faced forward. Lillian, rubbing her hand between Renee's shoulders, chose to ignore the implications of what they were saying. Max left the house, shutting the door behind her.

CHAPTER FOURTEEN

"RENEE LAMAR'S *previous forays into science-fiction - 2009's* Antimatter *and the film adaptation of* Luce Kanon *- may be wary to follow her back to space. Rest assured that Lamar's talent is finally allowed to shine through in a thinking-man's film that fully embraces science to explain its fiction, giving weight to the more fantastic elements of the plot. Lamar's Phoebe Kaiser will likely go down as this generation's Ellen Ripley.*"

Lillian had left by the time Max got back to the house. She'd gotten the number of Renee's dealer out of her phone and arranged a pickup. She bought what she could with the money in her wallet and made herself a receipt. There was a moment as she wrote the amount - four hundred - when she was amazed she just happened to have so much cash on-hand. She even had a little left over. Most of the money Renee paid her went directly into the bank, where it ceased being real to her. She wondered how much savings she'd built up, then dismissed the thought. As long as she was in the black, she didn't need to know an exact amount.

She had planned to just leave the pills and receipt on the kitchen counter, but she could see that Renee was still up and sitting in the living room, feet up on the divan so she could wrap her arms around her knees. Max knocked on the glass of the back door, and Renee waved her in without looking over her shoulder.

"I got fifteen pills," she said. "It was four hundred. You can just add it to my next check."

Renee turned around at that. "Four? For fifteen...? Who did you go to?"

"The guy in your phone."

"He gave you a deal."

Max said, "I guess. I can go put them in the teapot for you."

Renee faced forward again. "Why are you enabling me?"

"I'm doing my job. Protecting you. Let me know if you need any more."

"I'm leaving town for a while. Until the new year."

Max stopped on her way to the hall. Renee hadn't turned around, and Max briefly considered walking into the living room so she wasn't having a conversation with the back of her head.

"Rehab?"

Renee grunted. "No. I talked Lillian out of that. Just... going to get away. Obviously you're welcome to stay here. You can use the house as you see fit. No, um, no parties or anything like that. But if you want to invite Freddie over, by all means..."

"I don't think that's going to happen," Max said.

Renee said, "Thank you for getting me more pills."

"Sure. Let me know when you need more."

"Probably not before I leave."

"Okay."

Max went down the hall to the bedroom. She added the new pills to the teapot, replaced the lid, and used some toilet paper to clean up the excess powder. When she finished, Renee was standing in the doorway.

"Come with me."

"Okay," Max said. "Where do you need to go?"

"No, I meant..." She waved her hand out to one side. "I meant, the getaway. To recover, to get my head right. I know I said you could stay here, and that offer is still open, but this is another option. If you want. To come. I think if I go somewhere else, somewhere strange, all the anxiety and bad feelings that made me hire you in the first place will come rushing back and ruin any benefits I might be getting. We wouldn't have to be joined at the hip or anything, but I think just knowing you're nearby will be enough to keep me settled."

Max said, "Okay."

"Okay," Renee whispered, nodding slowly and smoothing her hands down the front of her slacks. Max didn't know if she was agreeing or just repeating.

"Where are we going?"

"I haven't figured that out yet. But I'll pay your way. It won't come out of your salary."

Max said, "Good to know. Yeah, sure. I'll come along."

"Great. I'll look into a few places and let you know." She looked at the teapot, seemed to consider saying something about it, but then pointedly looked away. She wrapped her arms around herself and lifted her chin. "The best thing about going away for a little while is you don't have to be yourself. I always check in under the name Flora Finch."

"Yeah, I've done that. Dora Lincoln."

"Oh. Sure. I-I forgot you... you were a boxer."

Max grinned. "Not quite the same level of famous as you, but yeah. There were concerns."

"I'll let you know when I've booked the place." She looked at the teapot again. "Thank you."

"Sure."

Renee walked away and left Max standing awkwardly in her bedroom.

They left two days later at the crack of dawn, hoping to beat traffic out of the city. Renee thought Max was surlier than normal, but she didn't know if it was a bad mood or just the early hour. Either way, they barely spoke as Max loaded their bags into the backseat of the Plymouth and set out. Renee was surprised by the transformation the car had undergone since the first time she rode in it. She hadn't paid much attention to it, but she knew that Max had spent most of her free time tinkering with it in the garage. Most of her paycheck probably went to replacing bits and pieces to revitalize its old skeleton.

"The car looks amazing."

"Thanks," Max said.

The sun was rising over the mountains, coloring the sky to reveal the ocean without blinding anyone who tried to appreciate the view like it did at sunset. Renee rested her head against the window and listened to the engine as Max drove.

"Music?" Max asked.

Renee looked at the console. "I didn't even know this thing

had a radio."

"Sure. And a tape deck. Part of the rebuilding process. It's not all cosmetic." She reached over and opened the glove compartment. Renee saw several cassette cases scattered within. "Take your pick."

"You're kidding me." She took out a tape at random and read the handwritten label. BEST OF QUEEN. "Did you make these yourself? Can people still make cassette tapes?"

"They're from high school. The car had a tape player when I bought it, I still had a bunch of these lying around, and I didn't feel like rebuying everything as a CD."

"Even that would be archaic. It's all streaming now. Digital." She took out another tape and put it in the slot without reading the label. "If this turns out to be no good, I have Spotify."

Their destination was a resort called Halcyon Retreat, a five-star hotel fifty miles outside of Los Angeles. It wasn't the most beautiful location unless you liked scrub brush and palm trees, but it was isolated and the staff was accustomed to celebrities who wanted to get away for a few days. She still used their fake names when she made the reservation, and the resort would keep up the ruse while they were guests.

They didn't beat traffic, so the trip took close to two hours. Regardless, the tape, full of songs from the late nineties that Renee had mostly forgotten, managed to last for the entire drive. Renee even found herself singing along to some of the songs and commenting on the bands.

"Whatever happened to the Wallflowers?" she asked as Max pulled into the resort's parking lot. It was mostly empty, which gave her hope that their getaway would be even more isolated than advertised.

"I'm sure they're still out there touring somewhere."

"I hope so. Jakob Dylan was hot."

Max parked and Renee went to check them in while Max unloaded the car. The resort was Y-shaped, with three wings branching off a spacious central lobby. She'd worn a hat with a large brim and Ray-Bans, but she had a feeling that the smiling mannequin behind the desk would have acted as if she was unrecognizable even if she'd gotten her hair and makeup done before she showed up.

"Good morning, ma'am, can I help you today?"

"I have a reservation for Flora Finch and Dora Lincoln. Should be two adjoining rooms."

His fingers pranced over the keyboard. "Yes, ma'am, I have you right here. You have rooms 8 and 9, which are down this corridor and located right near the pool. Your rooms are ready right now, in fact. Lucky!" He gestured to the right. "Are you Ms. Finch or Ms. Lincoln?"

"Finch."

He typed again, then withdrew two cards in paper sleeves. He placed them on the counter with a sheet for her to sign. She scribbled her name on the line and swept up the cards.

"Have a wonderful stay, Ms. Finch!"

"Thank you."

She met Max as she was coming into the lobby and traded one of the cards for her suitcase. They walked together down the hall, heads swiveling slightly to look at the advancing numbers. Renee wished she had asked how many of the rooms were occupied near theirs. It would be nice to know how isolated they would be. But it didn't really matter in the end.

"I guess this one is mine," Max said.

"We can swap," Renee said.

"Room's a room," Max said. "Wait. They're the same, right?"

Renee nodded. "No penthouses or suites here."

"Okay. Then whatever."

Renee went into her own room and placed her bag on the foot of the bed. She stretched her arms over her head and arched her back, wondering if a nap or a shower would be the better cure for the long drive. The curtain over the sliding glass door was open and she walked over to look out at the sprawling pool area. Six shaded cabanas stood on the opposite side of the still blue water. One of the cabanas was occupied, but there was a stillness about the grounds that, along with the lack of cars, made her believe the place was mostly deserted.

Lillian had argued for rehab. Take a few weeks, cut out the pills entirely, start the Benedict movie clean and clear. Renee argued that she had the oxy under control, and now she knew to avoid mixing it with other pills.

"You got into a fight with a dealer," Lillian had said, forgetting their cover word for it, "a scuffle bad enough that you hire someone to live in your house as protection. And a good thing you did, too. What would you have done if she hadn't been here? Hope Rand showed up for a nooner? You need to get your mind right."

"I can do that without giving up the pills."

The fight went out of Lillian after that, and she agreed to a compromise. She didn't have to start promoting *Queen Martyr* until February, so she had a month without any obligations. She could spend a few days or a couple of weeks at Halcyon, make it a retreat from her regular life in a neutral location where she could focus on the script and find her character. She needed to learn who Peggy Shippen was, what she believed, why she had pressured her husband to betray his country.

She went to her suitcase and unzipped it to find her e-reader. Not so surprisingly, there weren't any books written about Peggy herself. Her place in history was as a supporting character to the Traitor, the man whose name became synonymous with betrayal until a certain British actor hit the big time and made it palatable for Americans again. But she managed to find a few histories with chapters that focused entirely on Benedict Arnold's wife, and one novel which positioned her as a latter-day Lady Macbeth.

She wasn't sure why she invited Max along. Logically, it would have made more sense to leave her at home. She could watch over the place and make sure everything was okay. Being alone would have forced discipline on Renee and given her no choice but to research her upcoming role. There was also the fact Max had been a major factor in Renee's error in judgment. If Renee really wanted to heal, she would have put as much distance between her and her new protector as possible.

Renee looked at the door connecting their rooms. Maybe she was as dependent on Max as she was on the pills. Maybe the only way to get better would be to cut both loose and stand on her own two feet. The thought was as terrifying as taking off her parachute while standing in the door of a plane, and she was doubly scared by the idea Max had become so important to her in such a short amount of time.

She pulled the curtain shut and tossed her e-reader back onto the bed. She peeled off her sweater as she went into the bathroom.

Shower first. Soul-searching later.

CHAPTER FIFTEEN

"WHY HAS *no one ever let Renee Lamar play before? Miss Spells is unlike anything else in Lamar's admittedly-varied oeuvre, a silly adventure complete with one-liners, pratfalls, and physical comedy. A breath of fresh air following Lamar's recent releases, this is fun for the entire family.*"

Max had no idea what she was doing there. She sat on her bed, the open suitcase behind her still packed, and stared at the wall. When she was at Renee's house, she had a purpose. She was waiting to be sent on an errand or drive somewhere. Here, with Renee on vacation, she wasn't sure what was required of her or how she would fill her days.

She stood up and opened the sliding door that led out to the patio. Another pool, this one much larger than Renee's, and shining like part of the sky had fallen and embedded itself in the mosaic tile pattern. Max hadn't bothered to pack a swimsuit but the day was hotter than she'd expected. The urge to strip out of her T-shirt and jeans to dive into the water in her underwear was almost too tempting to deny. She might have done it if she hadn't seen the bare legs sticking out of a private cabana on the other side of the pool.

Max was about to turn around and go back inside when the other guest leaned forward to look around the edge of her cabana.

She was wearing a wide-brimmed hat and huge sunglasses which obscured much of her face. She was black, and her braided hair fell across one shoulder and rested on the bright red swim robe she wore. She smiled and held up her hand in a wave.

"Hello."

Max nodded. "Hi. I won't bother you, I was just..." She hooked a thumb over her shoulder, indicating her room.

"No, no, you don't have to run off." The woman had been holding a tablet, but she put it down and moved forward so she could see Max more clearly. "This place has been completely dead all morning. I'd welcome the company if you wanted to stay."

She hesitated, but then remembered what Renee had said about becoming someone else. This woman didn't know her and probably assumed she had paid whatever ridiculous price this resort asked for. As far as she knew, Max was rich and carefree.

"Sure. I can stay awhile." She walked around the pool. She took a seat on the lounge chair in the cabana next to the other woman. There was a moment where she debated whether she should use her real name or the pseudonym and, without consciously making a decision, the words "Dora Lincoln" came out of her mouth.

"Delia Hawkes." She rested her arms across her knees. "So what brings you to Halcyon, Miss Lincoln?"

"Traveling." She found it was easy to lie, to just give a random answer instead of the truth. She could keep it vague by giving misleading facts. "I needed somewhere close to Los Angeles and this place seemed good enough."

"I agree." Delia nodded and looked at the building as if she was only just now considering it as a place to stay. "I wanted isolated, but I wasn't expecting it to be quite so... desolate, I suppose is the word. I was starting to feel like I was in a *Twilight Zone*. Like I'd check out in a few days and stop for gas a few miles down the road, the clerk would see my room key..."

Max said, "Why, that place has been closed for ten years."

Delia grinned brightly. "Exactly."

"Maybe I'm part of it. Could be I'm the Devil in disguise."

"Hm, intriguing twist. I'll have to keep an eye on my soul." She chuckled. "Me, I'm a producer. I live in Chicago, but I need to have some face-to-face meetings with a few people, so I thought I'd live in luxury while I was out here."

Max said, "Can't fault you for that."

Delia had apparently been out in the sun for a while, and sweat was beaded on her forehead and upper chest. She looked away before she could be caught staring. The pool area ended in a wall high enough to keep away peeping toms but not so tall that it blocked the view of the nearby hills. Delia followed Max's gaze and smiled.

"I grew up in Kansas. First time I came out here, I told my friend who was showing me around that I loved looking at the mountains. It took her a second to realize I was talking about those things. Apparently those only count as mountains to us flatlanders."

"Mountains, hills. Either way, I don't want to climb it."

Delia laughed again. It had a nice sound.

"So what are you reading?"

"Nothing you'd care about. Contracts. Boring, boilerplate, but I have to make sure all the eyes are crossed and the tees are shirts."

Max furrowed her brow. "What?"

"Nothing," Delia laughed. "Contract humor. Lame contract humor. Forget it. You didn't tell me what you do for a living."

"Can't you guess?" Max asked.

"Oh, a game. Okay." She leaned forward and examined Max. "I don't recognize you, and I feel like you'd be famous enough for me to know you if you were in movies. You have some swagger. A lot of swagger, actually. Lots of confidence. Whatever you do, you're used to being in charge." She snapped her fingers. "You're a director. Not one of those boring blockbuster types. You do artistic shit, with a message. Movies that actually mean something to you. Am I close?"

Max laughed and shook her head. "Nowhere near."

"Then you don't have to tell me. I'm a firm believer in keeping some things secret. But for the record, whatever you do, you should be in charge. Remember that."

"I'll keep it in mind."

Delia looked past Max's shoulder and her eyes widened. "Oh shit. An actual celebrity sighting." Max turned but didn't see anyone. Delia pointed. "Renee Lamar was standing right there, watching us. She was holding the curtain open but she let it fall when I saw her. Damn. I love her."

"Looks like she's in the room next to mine," Max said, her voice neutral. "How about that, sharing a wall with a celebrity."

"It's probably a fifty-fifty shot in a place like this, with the price tag that goes along with staying here."

"True." Max could tell Delia was trying to find a way to relocate somewhere more private. Max could stay here and let that happen, but she was curious about why Renee had been watching them. "It was nice meeting you, Delia, but I have to get back to my room. Make a few calls."

Delia was obviously thrown. "Oh. Okay. Well, it really was nice meeting you. Hopefully we'll run into each other again before we leave."

"I'm sure we will."

She offered her hand, Delia shook it, and Max went back to her room. The connecting door between their rooms was open. She closed the curtain just in case Delia was the snooping sort and went into Renee's room. Renee was lying on the bed, arms out to either side, staring at the ceiling. She was in one of the hotel robes, and her wet hair spread out on the pillow around her head like a pool of liquid copper. Max walked across the room and leaned against the wall opposite the bed.

"You didn't have to leave," Renee said.

"I know." Max crossed her arms over her chest.

They were silent for so long that when the air conditioning clicked on, it startled them both. Renee sat up and smoothed her hands over her hair. She raked out the knots with her fingernails and eventually gave up, leaving it tangled. She dropped her hands in her lap and looked at the curtain as if she could see through it into the past.

"I don't care if you fuck people."

"I know," Max said again. "Because if you did, I'd quit. You can't dictate shit like that for your employees."

It was Renee's turn to say, "I know."

"Is that why you took the pills after the party?" Max asked.

"I didn't take *pills*," Renee said, "I took one pill that interacted with a different pill I had taken earlier. 'Taking pills' has connotations I don't want or need or... or feel are accurate."

"Fair enough," Max said. "Are you gay?"

"*No*."

"Bisexual?"

Renee opened her mouth to deny that as well, but it turned into a shake of her head and a downcast look.

"Do you want to fuck me?"

Renee bristled, her voice sharp. "That's... That is... inappropriate. I think you should leave."

Max said, "The whole point of coming here was to get away of who you are. Just for a little bit. To figure out what you need for balancing everything in your life. Despite that, you asked me to come along. Maybe you just wanted a driver, maybe there was another reason. Either way, I'm here. And you're paying me to help you out with whatever you need."

"I'm not going to pay you to have sex with me. God."

"I wasn't implying that." She thought back over what she'd said. "Okay. Maybe I kind of was. This is why I don't talk much. But the point is, I'm here. I want to help you. If you decide that would help you, then you could always just ask."

Renee repeated, "I think you should leave."

"Okay." Max pushed away from the wall and went back to the connecting door. "But just for the record, I'm not going to do anything with Delia. You don't have to worry about that."

"I wasn't... I don't care."

"Well, just so you know. Let me know if you want dinner."

She closed the door behind her when she left the room.

Renee stared at the wall. She didn't know why she freaked out. She only glanced outside to see if anyone else had appeared by the pool, and the first thing she saw was Max engaged in conversation with the stranger she'd seen earlier. It made her flashback to the last time she'd looked through a window and seen Max with a woman. This time it was just conversation, but she'd felt the same visceral reaction. It felt strangely like loss, or envy. Certainly not jealousy. Unless maybe she was jealous of the general situation. Sex with Rand was fine, but it was nothing compared to actual lovemaking.

And, what, did she think Freddie and Max were making love? No. It was clearly just two animals getting off together. So what was the craving for?

A *woman*, she told herself, the voice in her head sounding irritated that it had to be spelled out. *You haven't been with a woman in years, and you're craving that touch.*

She went to the minibar and searched the offerings. She took out one of the small bottles of alcohol and checked the label, wondering if she could mix it with her pills. She hadn't taken any since the Incident, but she didn't want to make it impossible. She certainly didn't want a repeat of what happened. Even if both times were complete accidents, rehab would come up again and this time Lillian wouldn't take no for an answer.

Renee put the bottle back and looked at her suitcase. The pills were there. Little white erasers which could take the edge off whatever she was feeling right now. She closed her hands into fists and rolled her wrists. Maybe just one. Swallowed instead of snorted, like it was an aspirin fighting off an impending headache. Or she could take advantage of the retreat's amenities. She could have stayed home if she was just going to sit in a dark room and get high. She could get a massage, take a yoga class, go for a proper swim in a full-sized pool. Hell, she could go out and fuck the woman by the pool herself.

Or you could just take your clothes off, go in there, and tell Max to do whatever she wants with you. Better yet, tell her to take you. You won't know when, you won't know how, but one day you'll turn around and she'll be there. And she'll take you and—

She swallowed the lump in her throat and pushed her hands though her hair. It was still wet from her shower. She paced in a tight circle and tilted her head back.

Finally, she went to the connecting door and stepped into Max's room. Max was sitting on the bed and looked up. Her expression didn't give anything away, no surprise or smugness, just an interest in what was about to be said. Renee was interested in that as well; she hadn't planned anything but now she either had to say something or look like a complete imbecile.

"They have some of my movies here." She gestured at the wall-mounted TV across from Max's bed. "On Demand. You said you don't watch movies so you probably haven't ever seen any of them. I thought you might want to watch one together. Or maybe a couple of them. So you could see... I don't know, so you can see what I do for a living."

Max said, "Sure."

"Okay then," Renee said.

The silence grew between them until Max said, "Did you mean right now?"

"I wasn't... um. Sure. Yeah. If that works for you."

Max looked around and seemed to realize there wasn't much else to spend her afternoon doing. She shrugged. "Sure."

"Okay. I'll... get some snacks from my room."

Max nodded and reached for the remote control. Renee turned and ducked back into her room. She had no idea if what she'd just done was a good idea or a disaster waiting to happen, but it was forward momentum. That was better than just spinning her wheels and seeing what else might send her into a skid.

CHAPTER SIXTEEN

"HOPELESS, NV *makes a valiant effort to be a pinnacle of Americana but unfortunately falls short of the mark. A solid Western with stellar performances all around, the movie is nonetheless weighted down by a rote plot and predictable action scenes. Renee Lamar and Randall Hurley do what they can to elevate an uninspired plot, but their lack of chemistry ultimately brings down their entire subplot.*"

When Max entered "RENEE LAMAR" into the search box, a column immediately appeared with a list of seven movies. Each one had a brief synopsis and a rating, the lowest of which seemed to be two and a half stars. Renee came back from her room with bags of snacks bundled in her arms and two bottles of beer dangling from the fingers of one hand. She had changed out of her robe into a sleeveless white top which draped over a pair of black leggings. She dumped the chips and cookies, held out a bottle to Max, and only paused for second before climbing into bed and settling with her back against the headboard. There was almost enough space between them for a third person.

Max gestured with the remote. "Which one do you suggest?"

"Depends on what you're in the mood for," Renee said. "*Holly's Holding it Together* got me a lot of critical attention, and Twitter said I was snubbed for an Oscar nomination. That felt pretty good. *Fire Hill Road* was my first movie. *Bedlam* is horror. I'd prefer not to watch myself get beheaded."

"Spoilers."

"Sorry," Renee said. She narrowed her eyes. "Wait. I was in the sequel... maybe I survived the first one. I just remember I had to get a plaster cast made of my head so one of the other characters could find it in their toilet."

"That one sounds classy."

Renee snorted a laugh. "Okay, start with *Past Lives*. That's an ensemble piece so it's not all about me. We actually won Best Ensemble for that from the Metropolitan Awards."

"Sounds good to me."

Max clicked on it and the movie began. "When was this?"

"Um... I think we filmed it in 2011, so it probably came out in 2012." She thought about it and then nodded more emphatically. "Yeah. 2012."

The movie began like a typical drama - Renee was a young attractive woman with a loving husband and a young son. She worked from home while he had some job that required him to wear a suit and carry a briefcase. On the day in question, she went to a hotel where she met a man with whom she'd been having an affair. She wanted to end things, he thought she was being ridiculous, and there was a moment when Max wasn't sure if things would end in sex or a fight.

Max didn't know how she would react if she had to watch a sex scene with Renee right next to her. She was even more concerned with how Renee would react. Surely, as tense as she was, she wouldn't have suggested a movie where she got naked. But if she wasn't sure about the release date, maybe she'd also forgotten about its rating.

Fortunately, the scene ended with a kiss. Renee's character fled the hotel room. It was later than she thought, so she texted her husband and asked him to pick up their son from school. "No problem." She went home and took a nap, waking up only when her cell phone rang. It was the police reporting that there'd been a car accident. Her husband and son were both dead on the scene.

"Shit," Max said.

"Yeah."

The rest of the movie focused on Renee's character going to a grief therapy group. She blamed herself for the accident. She said it was karma for the affair, the universe punishing her for taking her family for granted. The transformation the character had gone through was striking: from a typical suburban soccer mom to a silent, brooding woman with unwashed hair who smoked and drank too much.

"This won an award for ensemble...?" Max said.

"For the therapy group, yeah," Renee said.

"Well, you're the one doing all the heavy lifting."

Renee said, "Hm. thanks."

They watched the rest of the movie in silence. Renee's character started bonding with a man from group who lost his wife to cancer. He managed to bring her out of her shell to the point where she could function again. Max liked that it wasn't a romance, and the character's problems were nowhere near solved by the time the credits rolled. But the story had gotten to a point where the narrative could end with a sense of closure.

Max spent the last half hour distracted by thoughts of her own grief, the downward spiral after her final fight.

"Sorry," Renee said when Max returned to the list of movies. "Maybe we shouldn't have started off with such a heavy one."

"It's fine," Max said. "Just hit a little close to home."

"Oh." She could practically hear the unspoken question, the need to know more conflicting with the knowledge that it would be rude to press.

Max considered leaving it there, but the truth had to come out sooner or later. She couldn't think of a better opening than this.

"I killed a woman in the ring. Miriam Rudd. It was six years ago, Atlantic City, big fight. Lots of promotion. It was live on HBO. We were evenly matched, we were both popular, it was a big draw. I was the favorite to win, but I don't... Miriam was fierce and determined. I could see it in her eyes. We went seven rounds. In the eighth, I just decided I was going to end it. And I did."

Renee stared at her, speechless. Finally she said, "Wow. Was there... Did you have to stand trial o-or... how does that work?"

"We both signed waivers before the fight. Standard. As long as everything stays legal, and I did keep it completely legal, there was no liability."

"That's quite a thing to live with."

Max nodded and stared at the TV. She could feel the discomfort radiating off Renee and worried she might have ruined the mood. Whatever the mood might have been becoming.

Finally Renee broke the silence. "We should order lunch.

There's a room service menu in the nightstand. We can eat and then watch another movie, if you're up to it."

"Sure," Max said. "Turns out you're halfway decent."

Renee laughed. "Well, wait until you see me in something I won an award for."

Renee ordered a salmon hummus wrap, while Max got the turkey burger and fries. Renee added a bottle of wine just before Max hung up. She was worried about how they would kill time until the food arrived. But Renee went back to her room to "freshen up," and the food had arrived by the time she came back. The waiter set up the table near the sliding door, and Renee casually passed him a folded bill on his way out the door.

"How much did you tip him?" Max asked.

"Fifty."

"For this? God damn."

Renee shrugged as she took her seat. "It's expected in places like this."

"Maybe you should stay at cheaper places and pretend it's expected there, too. Those workers could probably use a fifty dollar tip, too."

"Maybe," Renee said. "But I can't exactly hope for privacy and anonymity the way I do here."

"Is that really so important? I know the fans and paparazzi are annoying, but if they go away, don't you go away, too?"

"Not so much. Maybe back in the days when it was all about getting coverage so people didn't forget about you. But these days, the real risk is overexposure. Everyone loves you for a little while, so every website carries your picture and follows your every move. Then people get sick of hearing about you, and now you're obnoxious. Anyway, these days the threat is less paparazzi and more stalker."

"Mm," Max said with a tilt of her head, accepting the argument. "You didn't mention any stalkers when you hired me."

"No stalkers. Just the threat of them always looming. If I stayed at a Best Western and some desk clerk called his buddy who posted a picture of me online, and some psycho happened to be in the area and wanted to be on the news..." She gestured vaguely. "It happened to Lana Kent, the singer at the Christmas party. About nine or ten years ago, she was stabbed in her apartment by a delusional fan. I'd just rather not tempt fate."

"I guess that makes sense."

Renee poked at her food. "It definitely wasn't in my plan when I decided I wanted to be an actress. I wanted to be famous, of course, but I didn't think anyone would care about me enough to hurt me. But the more attention I got, the more letters and emails came in with disturbing messages, eventually I realized there was a possibility that someone I'd never met would want to kill me.

"I actually started acting because I thought it would help me hide. I was horribly shy when I was a kid. No friends in middle school. In elementary school, every year my best friend was my teacher. In sixth grade, I got physically ill at the thought of leaving her class." Max grinned. "I'm serious. It was like I was changing mothers."

Max said, "And acting helped?"

"Acting was literally becoming someone else. Put on costumes, makeup, get your hair done, say words someone else wrote for you. And theater class was full of kids just like me. Well, not just like me, but close enough. We understood each other. It turned out I had a talent for it. It made me feel good. So I kept up at it. Mom paid for actual acting lessons, I went on auditions, and..." She waved her plastic fork. "Then it was kind of like a rolling stone, and I was just along for the ride."

"Hm."

"Lucky it did. I'm not really qualified to do anything else."

"Same with me and boxing, I guess," Max said. "I had to find something to do after I quit. You saw how well that was working out."

Renee said, "You found something. This. Protection."

Max laughed. "Yeah, protection. I'm a go-fer who doesn't mind the fact I might have to punch someone. I'm fine with it. I don't need some fancy job title. I know what I am. I'm happy to help you out."

Renee looked like she wanted to argue further, but she remained silent.

When they finished lunch, they went back to the bed with a glass of wine for each of them. Max picked up the remote and scrolled through the options again.

"*Holly's Holding It Together*," Renee said.

Max looked at the poster, which showed Renee in a red knit cap staring over her shoulder with a haunted expression. Her finger hovered over the Select button, her face twisted into a skeptical grimace.

"Really?"

"Trust me. You'll like it."

"All right..." Max clicked and put the remote control down.

Renee was the lead character in the movie, Holly Jarrett. She was freshly divorced, her job was hanging by a thread, and the opening scene took place after her beloved father's funeral. Her hair was shorter and styled poorly. She wore big eyeglasses when she wasn't out in public, in dark scenes where she bundled herself up in thick sweaters and read books or clicked around online. Max had to admit she maybe liked this version better than the real Renee. She seemed more human, more approachable.

At the end of the first act, the sword fell and her job was finally terminated. She went to a bar to drown her sorrows and ended up drinking the entire afternoon away. Eventually she was the only one in the bar, left with the bartender. They had a brief, dull conversation where Holly admitted that she had nothing waiting for her at home and no reason to wake up in the morning. The bartender pointed out that was a level of freedom most people would kill for.

"You've got nothing to lose and no consequences," he said. "So what's holding you back from doing whatever the hell you want to do."

"Nothing," Holly said, face brightening with the realization.

"So?" he said with a smile. "What do you want to do?"

She looked up at him, and the scene cut to the storeroom, where Holly was straddling the bartender and riding him hard enough to shake the shelves he was propped up against. Her sweater and bra was gone, and her bare breasts bounced with each thrust. She was sweating, grunting, teeth bared. She had one hand on the back of the bartender's head, eyes locked on his.

"Jesus," Max said.

"I figured I saw you in an intimate moment." Renee's voice sounded far away, almost meek, but it didn't sound like she regretted their choice. "Turnabout is fair play."

"I..." Max didn't know what to say. She felt like she should turn away, or grab the remote to fast forward, but she didn't do either and watched the scene play out.

Holly eventually finished and climbed off the bartender. She sat next to him to catch her breath while the bartender stared blankly ahead. She looked down at his lap and moved her hand over. There was obviously nothing graphic but it was clear what she was doing by the movement of her arm and the look on the bartender's face.

"No consequences," Holly said, eyes locked on the ceiling as she thought about the possibilities.

The bartender grunted his completion.

"Didn't think you did these kinds of movies."

"It's indie," Renee said. "It was my fourth big movie, right after I started making a name for myself. I didn't want to end up in a niche, so I was very careful about variety. I did small movies, thrillers, sci-fi, action. This was my Oscar-bait movie. 'A brave choice,' according to some critic or another. 'Utterly compelling.' I swear these guys all have a book of phrases they use. It's the same buzzwords in every review cycle. It boiled down to the fact I showed my tits in a movie that actually had a strong story and a quality director. That's the only difference between smut and art, in my opinion."

"Huh." Max's mouth was dry, and she was actually afraid she might be blushing.

The movie continued. Holly went home and showered - another nude scene, and Max forced herself to look at her face and not the water dripping off of Renee's... Holly's... small brown nipples.

"Do you want to touch yourself?"

Renee's voice was so quiet that Max thought she might have been quoting the movie. Then she realized she was referring to what Max had gestured at her through the glass at the Christmas party. She watched as Holly came out of the shower and wrapped herself in a towel. It was easier for her to think in complete sentences now that her breasts were covered up.

"No," Max said. "It's just... this is, ah, a hell of a movie to watch with the person who is naked on-screen."

"If you do want to touch yourself, it would be all right. I could leave." She took a sip of her wine, wet her lips, never taking her eyes off the screen. "Or I could stay."

Max looked at her. Renee looked away from the screen and held her gaze unflinchingly. Maybe it was the movie, maybe it was the fact they were on neutral ground and she felt like Renee's equal for the first time, but suddenly it didn't seem all that ludicrous. Max looked away first, losing the game of emotional chicken they'd been playing.

She slid her free hand across the mattress, to her waist, and unfastened the button of her jeans.

Chapter Seventeen

"WHAT WOULD *the Fifty Shades movies look like in the hands of a capable writer? Romantic and thoughtful sex scenes, characters who actually seem like living and breathing humans, and a focus on fetishistic sex that goes beyond 'tee-hee, we're being naughty!' As the title character in* Mistress Overdone, *Renee Lamar takes away the shame of sex and turns it into a beautiful, erotic masterpiece.*"

Renee silenced the mental *what am I doing* chant until it was just a faint murmur, the hum of an air conditioner in the other room or waves on the beach. She kept her hands folded on her stomach and her eyes on the screen, but she could see Max in her periphery, a long legs in jeans stretching up to a blurry image sitting beside her. The feet had been crossed but now they were parted, the outside knee slightly bent. Renee had heard the rasp of a zipper, and now she couldn't unsee the subtle movement of Max's right arm. Her hand was inside her pants, touching herself as instructed.

The movie was still playing on-screen. She didn't know why she'd insisted on it. She remembered every risqué scene, and maybe that was part of the reason she chose it. There was something unspoken between her and Max, a conversation which needed to happen about the moment they shared at the party. If they couldn't bring it up like adults, then this seemed like a good way to breach the subject.

But they weren't talking. They were just sharing a bed, Max touching herself while the version of Renee in the movie went down on a guy in a cab.

"Enjoying yourself?" she asked, keeping her voice low in case it cracked.

"It's not my preferred content," Max said, "but it's doing the trick. You..." Her voice cracked and she cleared her throat. "You have any lady friends in this?"

"No," Renee said. "Never. I don't do lesbian scenes."

"Huh."

Renee wet her lips. "There was a... a threesome in the script. The brunette at the beginning, Katie, and her husband, Joshua. I asked them to take it out."

"How graphic?"

"Not very graphic."

"Tell me."

Renee shifted against the headboard, the pillow bunching in the small of her back. "It was... it wasn't long after this scene. She thought her husband could hire me at his company, so I was having dinner at their apartment. We all got a little tipsy. By that point I was just fucking anybody who showed a slight interest in me. Joshua and I took the dishes into the kitchen, we accidentally bumped into each other, and I turned it into a kiss."

She glanced over at Max. Her head was tilted back, her eyes closed. She moved her hand in slow circles, the muscles of her forearm flexing and relaxing. Renee moved her hands down to her own lap, and her fingers conspired to pull her T-shirt up. She held it out of the way with one hand while her other slipped between her thighs. She pressed her legs together to trap it there.

"Katie walked in. We apologized profusely, but she said not to stop on her account. She came over to us. She kissed her husband. Then she kissed me."

Max said, "Then what?"

"It cut to the next morning. I was in bed with both of them~"

"No, not what happened in the script. What happened next?"

Renee closed her eyes. "They both undressed me. Emily... I-I mean Katie, Katie kissed my neck, while Joshua, um, his hands, he put his hands on my... hip. And he pulled me close to him, and Katie pressed against me from behind, kissed my neck, and I kissed him, and I... his cock, I took it out of his pants. Katie pulled up my skirt. Her hand... her hand went into my panties..."

Her hand was pressed flat against her crotch now. She kept it still, but her hips began moving. The bed protested under them, squeaking quietly in time with Max's rapid breathing. Renee looked at the screen and saw it was on another nude scene.

"Look... look at me."

Max opened her eyes and her grunt turned into a moan. "Oh, shit."

Renee's face burned hot and goosebumps rose on her arms as she stared at Max, watching her face as she came. She cursed again under her breath as she sagged against the headboard, sliding down with her eyes closed and her lips parted. After a moment she opened her eyes and looked at the TV, wetting her lips and sliding her hand up to rest on her stomach. Renee also moved her hand, resting it on her thigh.

"This is the second time I've seen you touch yourself without coming," Max pointed out. "Someone might think you have a problem."

"I..." Renee twisted her lips. "I can come."

"Then do it. Make yourself come for me."

Renee furrowed her brow and focused on the movie. The moment had passed, and now she regretted choosing this. She had two more sex scenes, two more scenes of nudity, and the thought of sitting through them was agony.

"If you don't, I will."

Renee snapped her head toward Max, stunned by the... offer? Threat? Her whole body warmed, and she clenched her teeth to stop herself from demanding Max leave, even though they were in her room. It wasn't like she was without options. She could tell Max to back off. She could stand up and go back to her room without saying a word. She could ignore Max for the entire rest of the trip and politely request she move out as soon as they got back to Los Angeles.

Instead, she decided to call Max's bluff.

Renee hooked her thumbs in her leggings, lifted her hips, and pushed them off along with her underwear. She kicked her feet until she was naked from the waist down. Part of her expected Max to shake her head, to back off, to admit defeat. Instead she rolled over and covered Renee's body with hers. They were briefly face-to-face before Max slid down. Renee held her breath as Max brushed across her breasts with not quite a kiss but not exactly an innocent touch, either.

Max settled between Renee's legs, moving them apart with surprising gentleness so she could have room to lie down. Renee stared straight ahead at a spot on the wall, then hissed through her teeth as Max's mouth touched her. Her hands flexed and then curled into fists, which she slammed into the mattress on either side of her hips. She was already desperately on edge from touching herself, and feeling Max's tongue on her was like throwing whiskey on a campfire. She moved her hands up to the back of Max's head, where she gripped the hair hard enough that it had to hurt, lifting her body up off the mattress. Max put one hand under Renee, cupping her ass, while the other hand...

"Fuck!" Renee shouted, the last coherent word out of her mouth for a few jumbled seconds. She lost track of time and her body. She forgot who was between her legs and that she was holding tightly to hair that could be pulled out by the handful, all she knew was the feeling of her orgasm. Her legs came up and closed around Max's torso, pinning her in place as Renee rocked against her tongue.

Eventually Renee released her, and Max wiped the back of her hand across her mouth as she moved to one side and resumed her position next to Renee on the bed. Renee was boneless, breathless, her eyes skimming the wall across from them for something, anything to focus on. She swallowed the lump in her throat and looked at the screen, where Holly was finally breaking down about her situation.

"That can be a thing that happened," Max said, "or it can be a thing that happens. Up to you."

"Right."

Renee wasn't entirely comfortable with the fact she was lying there so exposed, but her leggings had fallen off the foot of the bed. The idea of getting up, untangling them, and pulling them back on seemed so awkward that she decided to just stay like she was. It served a double purpose of being a power play, showing Max that she didn't have to put her armor back on immediately. She stretched her legs out and crossed her feet at the ankles. She was aiming for casual indifference but, when she looked at Max, she saw a knowing and smug smile on her lips.

They watched the end of the movie - Holly stopped sleeping around, stopped drinking, and started looking for work again - and ended up back on the main menu.

"Another?" Max asked.

Renee skimmed the titles on offer and didn't feel like sitting through any of them. "No, I think I'm worn out on watching myself for now. I should get back to my room and at least look at my lines for the Benedict movie." She scooted to the edge of the bed and stood up. Her shirt fell and covered her to mid-thigh, becoming a dress. She retrieved her leggings and balled them up rather than wrestling to get them back on. Her thighs were still wet, her legs trembling, and she knew she was too sensitive between her legs to even risk underwear.

"Would you like to meet for dinner?"

"Sure," Max said.

"How about, um, six?"

"Seven."

Renee said, "Okay. I'll... see you then."

She turned and went into her room and closed the door, closing her eyes as she sagged against it. Already the encounter was taking on the fogginess of a daydream. An especially vivid daydream. She put a hand between her legs and curled her toes in the carpet. She remembered Max's ultimatum, or promise, or whatever it had been.

This can be a thing that happened *or a thing that* happens. *Up to you.*

It was a small but important distinction, and one Renee didn't feel entirely competent to make just at that moment. She pushed her hair out of her face and realized she was sweating. She tossed her leggings onto the bed, peeled off her sweater, and went to take another shower.

She didn't have to make a decision right away, and the longer she put it off, the more confident she was that she would come up with the right answer. Right now she didn't trust her brain to make any choices more complicated than how cold to make the water when she got in the stall.

Max went to the bathroom and ran the water in the sink, holding her hands under the tap so it flowed over her fingers. She usually did this after a fight; it felt good and helped keep the swelling down. She didn't know why she was doing it now. She could hear the water running in the next room and tried not to imagine Renee in the shower. Despite everything they'd just done, she didn't know if their relationship had evolved to the point where she could fantasize without guilt. The masturbation and even the oral sex could have just been a stress reliever. No reason to expect it meant anything else, or that it would be repeated. She'd given Renee the option, and Renee had pointedly not chosen.

She brought her hands up and raked the wet fingers through her hair. She felt like the marathon started out as a test, or maybe a game of chicken. She wasn't sure which of them had been in charge. Maybe both, maybe neither. But she felt pretty confident that there hadn't been a winner. She didn't even know which of them would decide what happened next. Had Renee left the ball in her court? But Renee was still technically her employer, so really she should be the one dictating their next step.

Max sat on the foot of the bed. The TV was still showing the movie screen, with its selection of Renee's movies. She stretched for the remote and scrolled down to the title at the very bottom. *Fire Hill Road*, 2008, Renee's first movie. She clicked on it and fell back on her elbows as the credits rolled. At least part of the marathon's purpose had been so Max could see Renee's work. She had nothing else to do until dinner, so she figured she might as well kill some time by educating herself.

CHAPTER EIGHTEEN

"IN THE Myths of Last Tomorrow, *Renee Lamar gives us a glimpse of a quiet, normal post-apocalypse. The disaster has happened and life goes on, and Lamar turns an unfamiliar future into a relatable slice of life even when she's fighting to survive. An elegiac masterpiece that will be remembered for years to come.*"

Renee was aware of the sunlight on the curtains getting dim, but it didn't really occur to her that this meant it was getting closer to dinner. Closer to seeing Max again. She absorbed herself in and distracted herself with the script for the Benedict movie. *To the Inhabitants of America.* It was a hell of a title, based on an open letter Benedict Arnold wrote to explain his treason. She read the letter online, along with its responses, and then re-read sections of the script. She wanted to see Benedict as a person rather than a villain. The words "Benedict Arnold" didn't even sound like a name. It sounded like a title, like Peeping Tom. She needed to ground him in reality if she was going to convincingly play his wife.

The first step was changing her point of view. It was easy to look back two centuries and be shocked that anyone would betray America. But at the time, America didn't even really exist. From a certain point of view, the creation of a whole new country was the act of treason and Benedict was simply being a good and loyal Brit.

America was an idea, untested, built on shaky ground. History and *Hamilton* could make it look cool and inevitable, but if anyone tried to break away and form their own country... well, they would look like those guys who stock up on guns and build compounds out in Wyoming or took over wildlife refuges.

She had almost succeeded in forgetting what had happened earlier when Max knocked on the connecting door. She sat up straight on the bed, dragged out of the 1780s to present day. She saw how dark the room had become, the bed illuminated only by a single bedside lamp, and looked at the time to see she was over twenty minutes late to their dinner.

"Shit." She got off the bed and lurched to the door, grunting as blood rushed back into her feet. "Coming. Just a second."

She opened the door and was taken aback when she saw Max. Her hair was styled to make her look like an old-school movie star, side-swept and shining with a halo from the overhead light behind her. She was in a button-down shirt, and black slacks which were held up by a pair of suspenders. The sleeves were rolled up to show off solid, muscular forearms. She looked butch and beautiful, and the breath left Renee's mouth without the words she intended to say.

"You can cancel dinner if you want," Max said. "I just wanted to know for sure before I ordered something for myself."

"No, I... no, I just lost track of time." She looked down at herself and realized she was still in the pajama pants and T-shirt she'd put on after her shower. "Come in. Let me change into something more appropriate. You look amazing."

She stepped away from the door and went to her suitcase, which she still hadn't unpacked. Max eased into the room, almost as if she expected the invitation to be rescinded at any second. The script was still lying open on the bed and Max peered down at it, angling her head so she could see the pages correctly without picking it up.

"Is this the movie you're going to film next year?"

"Yeah. *To the Inhabitants of America*. It's a Benedict Arnold thing."

"Am I allowed to see it?"

Renee shrugged. "Sure, go ahead. I'll be right back."

She took her dress into the bathroom, considering how ridiculous it was to feign modesty after what she and Max had done. But there was a world of difference between seeing someone naked on a TV and being naked in the same room with the person. She doffed her after-shower clothes, did a quick smell test to make sure she hadn't somehow acquired a stink while reading her script, and put on the dress. She took a second to do her makeup, just enough that she wouldn't feel bad if Max thought this was a romantic situation, and went back out.

Max was still standing by the bed, but she'd picked up the script. Renee said, "What do you think?"

"Are you Peggy?"

"Mm-hmm."

"A lot of lines for you." She thumbed through the script. "Monologues."

Renee said, "Yeah, that's what Lillian promised me. But it's good?"

Max gave a non-committal tilt of her head. "It's fine. I'm not a good judge. It's as good as anything you did in the movies I saw today. Were you memorizing lines?"

"No, I have most of them already. Right now I'm trying to figure out who Peggy is. Working out how to inhabit her."

"If I do this, there's no going back."

It took Renee a moment to realize Max was reading from the script. It was one of Benedict's lines. She lifted her chin as she tried to recall where it fell in the story. When she spoke again, her voice had acquired a transatlantic accent. Not quite British, but posh and refined.

"No matter what decision you make, there is no 'going back,' Benedict. We are standing on a cliff and the only choice we have in the matter is whether we jump or are pushed. The world is going to change regardless of our actions here. We must take steps to ensure we can live with ourselves once the dust has settled."

Max looked up briefly, surprised by the accent, but she looked back at the page and found the next line. "People will see this as an unforgiveable betrayal. General Washington--"

"He's never truly cared about you," Renee snapped, moving around the bed to stand in front of Max. "You're an amusement in his eyes. Like a boy and his dog. But when you snap, he will not hesitate to strike you on the muzzle to keep you in your place. What kind of friend is that? What pathetic brand of loyalty requires you to remain under that viper's heel? It is time to earn your rightful place as a leader in your own right."

She knew what happened next. She watched as Max read the

stage direction, then raised her eyes from the page. It was just nine words - (Peggy cups the front of Benedict's trousers. She squeezes) - but those words carried a lot of weight in this moment. Until now, they had simply been reciting words, parroting a conversation off the page. She didn't have to follow through.

Renee stepped forward and pressed her hand against the front of Max's trousers. She cupped her between the legs and squeezed. Max didn't blink, but her upper lip curled slightly in response.

"Demand your due, my love," Renee purred, their lips almost touching. "Take your place in history."

Max flicked her eyes down to the page. When she spoke again, her voice was rough. "Perhaps I will take my place in this household."

"Take what is yours, my love."

Max threw the script onto the bed and gathered Renee in her arms. She pushed her against the wall, and crowded against her. Renee gasped when Max kissed her and moved one hand to the front of Max's trousers, fumbling with the button as Max grabbed her by the hips and jerked her sweatpants down. Renee twisted her hips to let them fall and turned her head to break the kiss, and then Max stepped back and spun her around. Renee put her hands flat against the wall and closed her eyes as Max pressed against her from behind. She jumped when she heard Max's voice against her ear.

"Do you have a dildo?"

"What?" Renee asked, momentarily confused by the question, and then she felt her cheeks burning when she realized the implications. "N-no, not here. I have a hairbrush."

"Where?"

"Suitcase. Inside. Plastic b-bag."

"Stay here."

And then Max was gone. Renee kept her eyes closed, one hand against the wall, and she moved the other hand between her legs. She heard water running in the bathroom and silently thanked Max for taking the precaution to wash it. It was hard to remember to keep breathing. She inhaled sharply every few seconds, and her face continued to burn, and then Max was back. She gasped in surprise and put her hand back against the wall.

"Move your feet apart," Max said, but Renee was already doing it, assuming the position, pressing back against Max's hips as if she expected to feel~

She cried out as the handle of the hairbrush pressed against her. She arched her back and felt Max's hand heavy on her shoulder. Renee reached down and used her fingers to guide the blunt end of the handle into her. Max's weight shifted and then she was inside. Renee bowed her head and cursed under her breath. The fact Max had to keep one hand on the brush made it awkward, took her dominant hand out of commission when there were a dozen other things Renee wanted it to be doing.

"Give it to me," she said.

"You want it?"

Renee grunted. "No, the brush, give me the... brush... I'll... give it to me..."

Max let go of the brush and Renee took it, hunching her shoulders. Both hands now free, Max got a good grip on Renee's shoulders and began thrusting against her. Renee matched her rhythm with the brush until it felt smooth and real, like it was Max inside of her. She threw her head back, hair flipping over her shoulder, and she looked behind her. Max was still fully dressed, but her pants were undone to maintain the illusion. Renee could see the dark elastic of her underwear and a thin strip of skin above it. Max moved one hand to Renee's hip and moved the palm in a wide circle, then scraped her fingernails over the same spot.

"Do it," Renee said, facing forward and holding her breath in anticipation.

Max spanked her, the first blow harder than Renee expecting. It made her cry out, but she bit her lip and moved the hairbrush faster.

"Harder," she said.

Max spanked her again, then again, and the noises coming out of Renee became more desperate, wilder, until at last she gave a final cry and came. Max held onto her hips and pressed hard against her, as if she was deep inside of her, and Renee knew she could feel every jolt and shudder of her orgasm as it wracked her body. She dropped the hairbrush to the ground between her feet, her toes curling. She put both hands against the wall, one on top of the other, and rested her forehead on them.

She could hear Max's breathing, almost as loud as her own, and she focused on it as an anchor to keep her grounded.

Eventually Max stepped away from her and bent down, picking up the brush and disappearing back into the bathroom. Renee swallowed and stood up as straight as she could. She turned her hand around and examined it to see why it was stinging so much.

The stiff bristles of the brush had left a patch of small pockmarks over the meaty part of her palm near her thumb. She pushed away from the wall and stood on unsteady legs for a moment, then peeled off her shirt and let it drop from her fingers as she walked naked to the bed.

Max appeared in the doorway to the bathroom and looked at her. Renee returned her gaze and then sat on the edge of the bed, swung her legs up, and stretched out. She could feel Max watching her, debating what she should do. Finally she went to the suitcase to return the hairbrush and sat on the other side of the bed. Renee looked up at her back, wishing she had taken her shirt off so she could see all her tattoos.

She sat there for close to a minute before she laid down as well. There was almost enough space between them for another person, a platonic barrier that seemed ridiculous given what they had just done. Neither of them spoke. The sweat dried on Renee's skin. She wondered if Max expected her to do something, to reciprocate. This was the second time Max had made her come without Renee doing anything in return. That was a pretty shitty ratio.

"I don't have a real... one."

Max turned her head on the pillow to look at her. Renee kept her eyes locked on the ceiling. She had one hand on her stomach, and the other on her hip. Her fingers were shaking almost imperceptibly.

"Do you want one?"

Renee wet her lips. "Yeah."

Max looked at the ceiling again. "I can get one."

"Tomorrow?"

Max said, "Yeah. Sure."

Renee nodded. "Okay. I'd like that."

More silence. Renee thought about dinner. She thought about the fact she was lying there naked with a fully-dressed Max right next to her. She thought about how the right thing to do would be rolling over, kissing Max, undressing her, making her scream, but she couldn't make her body follow through with it. She was terrified of taking that step. So instead, she just started talking.

"I use the name Flora Finch because she was a hugely popular vaudeville performer. She made almost two hundred shorts, which were... well, her era's version of blockbusters. She was part of the first-ever comedy film duo. And now, just over a century later, I can use her name to be anonymous, because no one remembers her. So

I use her name to remind myself that someday, maybe someday soon, a celebrity will check into a hotel as Renee Lamar and no one will care."

"Those old movies are lost," Max said. "Your movies are on TV at the press of a button. Not to mention all over the internet. Things are saved now. The good thing is that people will definitely remember you. The bad thing is they'll never forget you. Even if it's just as that lady who used to be in movies."

"I don't know if that's comforting or depressing."

"Maybe that's why you take the pills."

Renee was startled by the blunt appraisal, but it was a fair point.

Max sat up and put her feet back on the floor. "I'm hungry. I'm going to order some room service. Do you want to join me?"

"Yes," Renee said, having somehow become the monosyllabic one in their relationship. "Caprese salad, please."

Max nodded and went into her room. A few minutes later, Renee heard her calling in the order. Judging by how quickly their lunch order arrived, she had fifteen minutes to get up and get dressed before the waiter showed up. She would have to hurry if she wanted to shower and put on a little makeup. But she could lie there a bit longer and recover, and try to come to terms with what had just happened.

CHAPTER NINETEEN

"TAUT, GRIPPING, *and thoroughly entertaining,* A Clever Hawk *is an intelligent spy thriller that trades gadgets and explosive action scenes for clever manipulations and mental grappling. Renee Lamar is a stand-out in a cast full of heavyweights, mesmerizing in her role as a grandmaster playing a game on a global scale.*"

Max woke early, just as the sky was beginning to erupt in pastels, and drove to an "adult boutique" she'd found online the night before. That was the thing about America; even in the middle of nowhere, you were probably less than twenty minutes away from a smut shop. Renee's room had been silent and still when she put her ear to the door and she decided not to disturb her. Renee had been quiet over dinner, distracted to the point of practically being in a different room entirely. Max watched her for signs of the wrong kind of discomfort, any evidence that they'd gone too far or she was regretting the events of the past day, but it seemed to be closer to anxiety. Uncertainty about what would happen next, where they would go from here, rather than wishing she could reverse time.

So Max carried on with the plan. The boutique was open twenty-four hours, but she was still surprised to find several cars parked outside the unassuming gray building at such an early hour. A couple at the back browsed the lingerie racks, and a man with a baseball cap pulled low over his face drifted along the DVD display. She tried to avoid him as much as possible. She found a faux-leather harness that came with a realistic dildo that seemed like it would fit their needs perfectly. She wasn't a fan of lifelike toys, but she had a feeling it would make Renee more comfortable than any of the smooth, neon-colored versions.

The girl behind the counter had a textbook of some sort propped against the cash register and reluctantly pulled herself away to ring up Max's purchase. Max glanced at the colorful design of the girl's shirt, and it took her a moment to recognize the name emblazoned below the collar: LUCE KANON.

"Are you a fan of the comic?"

The girl looked at Max, looked down at her shirt, and shrugged. "It's dope. You read it?"

"No, I have a friend who is a fan. More a fan of the movie, I think."

"Oh god, that thing was a piece of crap. What a total mess. They never should have let Clarke put his stink all over it. Did you see it?"

"I don't really go to the movies."

"Well, you can skip this one. They straight-washed Luce and completely missed the point of why people love the book in the first place. Hollywood, right? But definitely check out the comics."

"I'll do that."

Max thought about the conversation as she drove back to the retreat. She wished there'd been a way to ask about Renee specifically, but she didn't feel comfortable floating her name in an establishment like that. There was little to no chance the girl would have made the connection and assumed who the sex toy was going to be used on, but it was still better to be safe than sorry. She would like to know if the girl made an exception. "The movie sucked, but she was actually really good," something like that.

Famous didn't always mean popular. What if the public loathed Renee? It was possible, and it would explain why she was so damned scared all the time. But everyone at the party seemed to like her well enough. Everyone could make one bad movie, and weren't all comic book movies pretty lousy? She'd seen a lot of superheroes the past few Halloweens, so maybe there'd been a paradigm shift at some point.

It didn't matter, she decided, accepting the fact her curiosity was based on a general interest in Renee. She wasn't sure she wanted that. What they'd done the day before was fucking. Nothing emotional, not even reciprocation on Renee's part. It was stupid to slip into a relationship mentality, but that was what her question at the store had been.

She shunted away the thoughts as she crossed the lobby, ignoring the chipper "Good morning, Ms. Lincoln!" from the desk clerk. She went into her room, took the box out of the bag, and placed it on the bed. She stared at it for a moment, then knocked on the connecting door.

It opened so quickly that she wondered if Renee had been lying in wait. Her hair was still tangled from sleep, a paler red than she was used to seeing. She wasn't wearing makeup and a shadow of freckles spread across the bridge of her nose. She was also wearing a pair of big eyeglasses that Max had never seen before.

"Morning." Renee reached up, maybe to take off the glasses but instead pushed her hair back off her forehead. The move revealed another field of freckles. "Um. Breakfast?"

"If you want," Max said. "I just wanted to let you know I got the thing."

"What thing?" Renee glanced past Max and saw the box sitting on the bed. "Oh, Jesus, the thing."

"I don't want to pressure you. We can order breakfast~"

Renee cut her off with a wave of her hand. "I-I don't... I don't, um... Let me take a shower? Give me twenty minutes. And... and then... come into my room."

"Okay."

Renee nodded and stepped back into her room, shutting the door. Max stepped back and went to retrieve the box. It appeared she had some time to kill, and there was a chance it would take her the full twenty minutes to figure out the harness.

Renee pressed her hands against her face and let the water cascade over the top of her head. She was trembling again, and it was hard to catch her breath. She laid awake most of the night reliving what had happened with Max. The masturbation, the oral sex, the hairbrush. With the lights off and in a strange bed, it was easy to pretend it was something that happened to a character she was playing. It had been amazing and thrilling, and she came harder than she ever had with any other partner, but maybe that was because she could pretend it wasn't real. She was here, she was in this unfamiliar place, and Max was... Max was...

Max was masculine, Max was rough and silent, Max was a woman, Max took charge but asked consent, Max was everything Renee had been unconsciously fantasizing about without ever admitting it. And now she was in the other room, and she had... she'd bought a...

A shiver ran through her. She reached out and turned off the water, stepped out of the stall, and looked at the travel bag next to the sink. She hadn't touched it since they arrived, but now... she was so on edge, she could use something to bring her back down to earth. She unzipped the bag, took out her pills, and used the water glass to crush one. Swallowing them whole had long ago stopped being an option. Now to get the full effect, she had to take it this way. She didn't mind. It was a commitment, it was a ritual, and doing it every time she wanted a hit made the pills mean something.

She put on a T-shirt and a pair of lacy boyshorts. She came out of the bathroom with her hair still wet and stopped short when she saw Max standing next to the bed. She was still wearing what she'd had on earlier: jeans and a V-neck shirt. Her hair had been washed but it still fell wild across her forehead.

"Oh." Renee swallowed. "I thought you were going to put on the..."

"I did."

"Oh." Renee dropped her eyes to the crotch of Max's pants. Now she could see it, the awkward bulge at the front. "How are you... i-it's not..."

"Boxer briefs," Max said. "I thought you'd want it as authentic as possible."

Renee said, "Yeah," and her voice was rough. "Would you take off your shirt?"

"You don't have to make it a question."

Renee took a deep breath. "Take off your shirt. Show me your tattoos."

Max crossed her arms, grabbed the hem of her shirt, and pulled it over her head. She was wearing a sports bra, but the tattoos were exposed enough for a good examination. Renee stepped closer. The lights were off and the curtains were mostly closed, but there was enough of a gap to let in some of the early morning sun. When Renee was close enough, she put out her hand and touched a random curl of ink on Max's shoulder. She realized she was holding her breath and forced herself to release it, moving the pad of her finger down the line, following the curve of Max's shoulder.

"What does it mean?"

"Nothing, to you," Max said.

"That's fair."

Renee acted on impulse and bent down, placing a kiss on a burst of yellow that took up most of Max's shoulder. She opened her mouth and traced the tattoo, moving up as her hand moved down. She skipped the strap of Max's bra and kissed her neck, sucking as she stepped closer, her free hand going around Max's waist to pull her close.

"You've done this before, right?" Max asked. "Other women?"

"Yes." She straightened so she could see Max's face. "But I don't want to do what I've done before. I want to... I want you. To be with you, whatever that entails."

Max took Renee's right hand and guided it between them, made her cup the bulge at the front of her pants. Renee held her breath and squeezed, not breaking eye contact as she brought her other hand around and unfastened the button. Max remained unblinking as the waistband of her underwear was pulled down and the dildo swung free.

"Tell me if I should stop."

Renee nodded. And then, in a blur of movement, she had been turned and bent over onto the bed. She bent her elbows underneath her as Max yanked her shorts down. Renee pushed herself up onto her elbows and closed her eyes in anticipation, glancing over her shoulder to see Max spreading some lube onto her fingers before she dropped the bottle onto the floor. She stroked it into the toy and lifted it until Renee felt the tip against her. Renee faced forward again.

"Yes, sir," she said, and then cried out. She hunched her shoulders and curled her fingers in the sheet. Max started with slow, measured movements. She kept one hand on Renee's hip while the other pushed up under her shirt, following her spine and then letting her fingernails rake back down. Renee's body responded like a cat, her back arching as she pushed back to meet Max's forward thrusts.

"Faster?" Max whispered.

"Yes, sir," Renee said again.

Max complied, and she moved both hands to Renee's hips. Renee dropped her head and closed her eyes, moving her legs further apart. She loved how Max's fingers stung her skin, but at the same time she was aware that she would be on camera for interviews about *Queen Martyr* in the next few weeks.

"Don't bruise me, sir," Renee murmured, her lips barely moving.

"Hand me that."

Renee lifted her head, glanced back, and followed the line of Max's finger to the bathrobe lying discarded on the edge of the bed. She grabbed it and flipped it back, and Max caught it. She remained still, the toy still fully inside of Renee. She did something with it and then Renee felt the soft brush of terrycloth over her hip. The unexpected softness made her twitch and tremble as Max threaded the belt around Renee's waist.

"What are you doing?"

"Shh."

Max reached under Renee and then, one end of the belt in each hands, wrapped the strip of cotton around her hands like reins. She bent her elbows and the belt pulled Renee back as Max thrust her hips forward.

"Ahh, fuck," Renee moaned. "Please ride me, sir."

The bed became the loudest thing in the room, though Renee could hear each of Max's grunts like they were inside of an echo chamber. Renee loved the way the belt pulled her, loved how it felt like her whole body was being moved at once. It was almost like being on a swing. She could feel Max's strength in the tautness of the material against her stomach.

"Touch yourself," Max said.

Renee slid a hand over the mattress and reached between her legs. Two fingers brushed her clit and she hissed through her teeth.

"Do you like this?"

"Yes, sir, fuck me," Renee grunted.

Max said, "I like the please."

"Please, please, fuck me, please," Renee chanted.

"Sir."

"*Sir*," Renee cried, throwing her head back, dragging out the word as she came. Her knees locked and her free hand pulled on the sheet hard enough to make it come untucked at the top corners. She stretched out, the toy falling out of her, and she put a hand over her mound as protection as she settled onto the mattress. She looked back without lifting her head and saw Max looking at her, the wet cock sticking out of her underwear.

Max said, "You okay?"

"Mm-hmm." Renee rolled over onto her back an held out a

hand. "You."

"What?"

Renee flicked her fingers. "Your turn. Come here. I'm not... I don't know if I can do what you need, but you can use me however you need to get off. I want you to."

Max remained where she was for so long that Renee thought maybe she was offended. But she finally pushed her pants off, pulled at a strap on her harness, and let the toy fall away. She pulled off her sports bra and Renee saw her completely naked for the first time. She wet her lips and held out her other hand, inviting Max to climb on top of her.

Max's knees dug into either side of Renee's right leg as she straddled her. Renee sat up and they looked down where their bodies met, shifting their weight until Max found a comfortable position on Renee's thigh. She began to grind, and her thigh brushed against parts of Renee that were still sensitive from her orgasm. She hissed and stiffened.

"Okay?" Max asked.

"Mm-hmm, don't stop."

"Sir," Max said.

Renee shook her head and put her arm around Max. She spread her fingers out and pulled Max to her, lifting her body to match their movements. She dropped her head against Max's chest.

"Max," Renee said, eyes closed. "Don't stop, Max. Come for me, please."

"Almost," Max said.

"Can I kiss you?"

Max grunted instead of answering, so Renee lifted her head. Her lips glanced off Max's, the angle awkward, but Max twisted her head and found her. She didn't break the kiss as she leaned forward, forcing Renee down onto her back. She changed the angle of her hips and Renee gasped again, tried to squirm away and then twisted her body to meet Max's thrusts, holding on tight as she was rushed into a second, unexpected orgasm.

She felt Max shuddering in her arms and knew she had come as well, but her mind was too scrambled from what had just happened to process it properly until Max lifted off of her and moved to the side, lying on her stomach on the other side of the bed. Renee's skin was suddenly too hot, and she felt sweat beading on her forehead, upper lip, chest.

"The 'sir' just comes out sometimes," Renee said.

"Mm-hmm," Max responded.

"It's a submissive thing. Sometimes I say other things."

Max turned her head to face her. "Like what?"

"Officer. Daddy."

"I wouldn't have liked daddy."

"Good to know."

"Is it?" Max said.

Renee looked at her, examining her expression. "For next time."

"For next time," Max repeated.

"This is going to happen again. For as long as we're here. And when we get home, we can figure out what happens long-term." She looked away long enough to locate Max's hand, linking their fingers together. "If that's okay with you."

Max nodded. "Sure. It's okay with me. Might as well get my money's worth for that strap-on."

Renee closed her eyes and laughed.

CHAPTER TWENTY

"TO TELL *the harrowing true story of a soldier disfigured by a roadside bomb, Renee Lamar spends the majority of* Burning Without Flame *with her face hidden under bandages and heavy prosthetics. Her eyes tell the full story, however, revealing an inner struggle that no dialogue could hope to convey. Lamar makes a case for another round of nominations here.*"

They fell into a comfortable routine for the rest of the week. Breakfast together, sex, working on the Benedict script, lunch, then Renee would take a nap and Max would go for a run or a few laps in the pool. Then dinner and more sex. They occasionally watched one of Renee's movies, but those afternoons quickly ended up the same way as their first movie marathon.

Max was surprised at how voracious Renee had become. She was submissive for the most part, but occasionally she would take control in surprising ways. She once covered Max's mouth with her hand, refusing to let her speak until they both came. Another time she grabbed a handful of Max's hair and pulled hard enough to hurt.

Sometimes they roleplayed. Max was a police officer, Max was a doting fan, Renee was a Presidential candidate who had hired Max for the evening. It wasn't what Max was used to, and it was nothing she would have expected to feel comfortable with, but given that acting out the Benedict script had taken them down this road, it only seemed natural.

On their last night at the resort, after a spirited session in which Renee was a starship captain and Max was an alien ambassador, they were lying together under the blankets in Renee's bed when Max asked, "Do you like roleplaying because you're an actress, or is it the other way around?"

"I always liked pretending to be other people." Renee dragged the tip of her middle finger over the curve of Max's hip. "I guess both things sprung from that aspect of my brain. I put on costumes and pretend in front of the camera for the same reason I like to make up stories in bed."

"Well, we've got one more night here," Max said, shifting to cover Renee's body with her own. "Is there any role we didn't get around to that you want to check off the list?"

"Really? Again? You're not sore...?"

Max shrugged. "Soreness fades."

"In that case," Renee said, sliding her hands lower on Max's body, "there is one thing I've been wanting to try..."

"It really doesn't feel like Christmas in the desert," Renee said.

Max glanced over at her, seeing past her to the warehouses and restaurant signs poking up over the side of the highway. She faced forward again. "Maybe it only feels wrong because of the things you did to Mrs. Claus last night."

Renee snickered and stretched, folding her arms against the roof of the car. "Maybe. But the lack of snow is definitely not helping."

They were almost back to Los Angeles, back to Renee's real life and the daily grind of being an actress. Lillian had already texted and emailed at least four times to confirm interviews which had been set up. Apparently the entertainment world kept chugging along even two days before Christmas. Renee had the script for *Queen Martyr*, the movie she was supposed to start promoting soon, to remind herself of the finer points of the story so she could answer any questions which might come up on the press tour.

"Well, you know who definitely never saw snow in his lifetime? The birthday boy. Jesus never had a white Christmas."

"Touché." Renee looked out her window, lifting her chin so she could see down to the surface streets. "It'll be nice to be home, though."

"Yeah? Feeling relaxed?"

"Well, I'm definitely not going to panic if I see you fucking Freddie McCoy again."

Max said, "You're welcome to join in."

"Don't tease. I can call her right now, have her waiting at the house by the time we get there."

There was a car parked in the driveway when they arrived but, judging by the word Renee said under her breath, Max assumed it wasn't Freddie. The relaxed mood Renee had enjoyed for the entire ride evaporated in an instant. Max pulled into the garage and Renee unbuckled her seatbelt before the car was even in park.

"Wait here," Renee said.

She was gone before Max had a chance to protest. She got out of the car and followed Renee as far as the kitchen, stopping where she could hear what was happening in the living room without being seen. Renee was in the middle of saying, "What the hell are you doing here?" Max leaned her shoulder against the fridge and listened.

"God, you're a sight for sore eyes," her guest said, ignoring the question as if she hadn't spoken.

Even if Max hadn't recognized his voice from their previous encounter, she had just heard him in *Hopeless, NV*, which they had watched in Renee's room in between rounds. It was Rand Hurley, Renee's love interest in the movie who became her fuckbuddy in real life. He was also inconsiderate in bed, a jerk in real life, kind of a dummy, and had a habit of taking things that didn't belong to him when he left the house. When Max asked why he was worth the trouble, Renee shook her head.

"He's not so bad when he's not talking," she said, "so I just gave his mouth other things to do."

His mouth was not occupied now, unfortunately. "You look amazing, babe. Getting away really agrees with you."

"You haven't been here the whole time, have you?"

"No. Lillian told me you were coming home today. I called her because I missed you. I wanted to see you."

Renee said, "Look, I'm sorry, but all I want to do is take a shower and lie down for a nap."

Rand's voice became seductive. "That sounds great, baby. But what do you say I draw you a nice bubble bath... give you a backrub... and we'll see what happens with that nap, hm?"

"I just want to rest," Renee said.

"I'll make you so relaxed…"

Max couldn't listen to any more. She stepped around the counter and saw Rand and Renee standing in the living room. He had his hands on her shoulders, far enough apart that even a high school dance chaperone would have been fine with it, but Renee had her head bowed in a posture of defeat that Max despised. Rand looked past Renee and frowned.

"She asked you to go."

Rand dropped his hands to face Max completely. "No, actually, she didn't."

"Then I'm asking you."

He stepped around Renee. "And who the hell *are* you, anyway? You don't get to dictate who she spends time with. I think you've been hanging around here long enough. You think you're the first con artist who has taken advantage of Renee's good nature? You think she's going to let you leech off of her forever?"

"I think I saw the real Renee," Max said, and nodded at Renee. "And I know that isn't her. That's someone who is too weak or polite to tell you to get the hell out of her house. So I'm doing it for her. Because that's who I am. That's what I do."

Rand worked his jaw and stared at Max, unblinking. "Okay, honey, whoever you are, it's clear one of us has to go, and I've been around a hell of a lot longer than you. So…"

Renee said, "Rand, go."

He turned to her. "What? What the hell are you saying?"

"Max, please. Show him out."

Max stepped forward and held her arm out toward the door. "You heard the lady."

"And don't come back," Renee said. "Whatever we had, it's over. You're not welcome in this house anymore."

Rand aimed a finger at Max. "This is you. Wherever you took her--"

"Get that finger out of my face."

"--you brainwashed her or, or drugged her or something."

"One more time," Max said calmly.

"You want to cut off her industry contacts, her friends, people who get her work--"

"Get your finger out of my face, Mr. Hurley."

"Make me!" he shouted.

Max took hold of his finger and broke it as casually as someone might tear a number from a bulletin board. He went down on one knee, and Max thrust her hand forward against his chest. It was a glancing blow, power-wise, but it was enough to suck the wind from him when combined with the shock of the pain she'd just sent through his hand. She grabbed a handful of his shirt and forced him back onto his feet.

"You were asked to leave private property. We asked politely. Feel free to file a police report, but I'm fairly certain you won't come out looking like the hero of that story." She opened the front door and shoved him out, just hard enough to get him over the threshold but not so hard that he would fall down the stone steps. "Renee will call you if you're ever welcome back in her house. But I wouldn't wait by the phone."

She slammed the door and twisted the lock. The adrenaline was fading, and it occurred to her that Renee might not entirely agree with everything that had just happened. Yes, she wanted Rand to leave, but Max's actions could seriously have burned some vital bridges for her career. She stepped away from the door and went back into the living room. Renee hadn't moved, but she'd turned her head slightly to look out the front window. The blue of the sky and ocean reflected in her eyes, making them seem to glow blue, and Max understood how this woman became a movie star.

"I'm sorry if that was–"

"Take me."

Max blinked. "I'm sorry."

Renee looked away from the window and focused on Max again. Her face and throat were flushed and she was breathing heavily. Her fingers were wrapped around her thumbs, and she was swaying on her feet.

"Take me," she said again. "Right now. I want you to take me."

"Rough?" Max said, already unbuttoning her shirt as she crossed the room.

Renee lifted the hem of her shirt, unbuttoned her pants, and stepped out of her shoes. "Yes."

Max cupped Renee's face. "Safe word."

"No."

Max's hand slipped to Renee's throat. "Yes."

Renee surrendered and said, "Ketevan."

With that established, Max tightened her grip and kissed her, pushing her across the room until she hit the wall. Renee clung to her, one hand on the back of her head while the other snaked under her arm. Max put her hand on the top button of Renee's blouse and pulled back just enough to see her face. Her eyes were closed and she was shaking.

"Should I–"

"Stop asking questions and take me," Renee said. "Whatever that means to you. I want it."

Max jerked her arm, pulling off half the buttons of the blouse with the move. She felt the tiny little stings as they ricocheted off her chest and skittered across the floor. Another pull, lower on the shirt, got it completely open. Renee pulled it off and Max looked over her shoulder at the window. The lawn was steep enough that no one on the sidewalk could see in, but she didn't want to take a chance Rand would come back.

"On the floor," she demanded.

Renee complied immediately, sliding down the wall and stretching out where she would be blocked by the couch. Max stood over her, staring down as she undid her belt and took off her pants. Renee lifted her arms over her head, stretching and twisting, moving her legs apart in anticipation. Max knelt down in the V made by Renee's legs and bent forward. She wrapped her right hand around Renee's throat and put her left hand against her own crotch before moving forward.

Renee's eyes were wide. She nodded her head once, and her eyes rolled back as Max pushed two fingers into her. This was nothing like their encounters at the resort. Not even in their wildest games had they pushed the line so far to roughness. Max watched Renee's lips carefully for a hint she was even trying to speak, to form the word she'd assigned to mean things had gone too far.

"Is this what you wanted all along?" Max asked, thrusting hard enough to make Renee's entire body jerk. "Someone to hurt you... just enough? Someone to take control...? Someone who will hurt you but stop when you say stop?"

"Yes," Renee croaked.

"I lost control once," Max grunted.

"Ng... Trust you..."

Max held Renee's gaze. The skin of Renee's throat was soft under her fingers, horrifyingly fragile. She could feel blood pulsing under her thumb. She tightened her grip and Renee made a weak, desperate noise. But her parted lips remained still. A small part of Max's brain told her that the strange word - Ketevan - could almost be pronounced without moving the lips at all. She should have made Renee choose something that would require pursing her lips, using her tongue. A word with a P, a B, an L or an F. Renee could be hissing 'Ketevan' without Max realizing it.

"You're going to come for me," Max said.

Renee closed her eyes and lifted her chin.

"You're going to come for me right now." She released her grip and Renee gasped. Max moved her hand up into the thick, red hair at the back of Renee's head and pulled. Renee cried out. "Say it."

"I'm going to come for you, Max," Renee whimpered in a rough voice that cleared with her next cry of pleasure. Her body convulsed and she reached down to grab Max's forearm, guiding her through the last few strokes. Max watched Renee's throat, every small twitch of her face, the way her eyes squeezed shut and then flew open to stare at nothing above her head.

When she was lying still on the floor, Max released her handful of hair and stroked Renee's throat with her fingers.

"God, I hope it doesn't bruise..."

"There's always makeup." Her voice was rough, and she cleared her throat in an attempt to get rid of the gravel. "Thank you for that."

Max lifted herself up and moved to the side, stretching out next to Renee on the floor. She looked at her fingers, still wet, and brought them to her mouth. Renee watched her and shivered again.

"You're sure it was okay?"

Renee nodded. She touched her neck, starting just below her chin and stroking downward. Her shoulders jumped when she reached the spot where Max's fingers had dug in. "I wouldn't want that every time, of course. But in that moment, after watching you... be so... It happened after you attacked that paparazzo a while back. You broke his phone. It made me wet." She cleared her throat again. "If we have a little warning next time, maybe we could actually use... things."

"The cock is still out in the car."

"No. I meant... handcuffs. Or. Whatever."

"Ah. We could do that, too."

Renee coughed. She stroked her throat. "Maybe you're right. Maybe this whole time I've been looking for someone who scares me a little, but that I also trust. And maybe you've been looking to be that person."

"I didn't even know who you were until—"

"No, not for me specifically. You hurt someone so badly that you stopped fighting. You scared yourself. You need someone who trusts you enough to let loose with. I can be that person. I want to be that person. And it seems like we'd both get something out of it."

"I'm not going to hit you."

"No. No hitting. But maybe other stuff."

Renee pushed herself up and straddled Max's thighs, unbuttoning her pants. Max watched her tug down the zipper, wet her fingers, and push the underwear out of the way.

"What are you doing?" Max asked.

"When this started, I promised myself I wasn't going to just take. So this is me... returning the favor. Any requests, Miss Reszke?"

Max put her hands behind her head and smiled. "Yeah. Go slow."

CHAPTER TWENTY-ONE

"RENEE LAMAR takes another breather in Bedding Seattle, a lightweight comedy in the wake of her award-winning portrayal of Colonel Caruso. This role won't win her any awards, but she still brings her considerable talents to this fun, silly, sexy romp. And it's certainly refreshing to see Lamar enjoying herself on-screen for a change."

"So what is Ketevan?"

It took Renee a moment to remember where Max had heard the name. They were both dressed again. Max was lying on the couch, facing the window, and Renee was sitting at the kitchen counter with her laptop so she could catch up on the emails she'd missed during their getaway.

"Ketevan was a 'who'," she said. "A Georgian queen. Ketevan the Martyr. She was held prisoner by the Persians who demanded she convert to Islam. She refused, even though she was brutally tortured. They, um, well, they did awful things to her and eventually threw her body to the beasts. Lions, probably. I played her in the movie I'm going to start press for in January. *Queen Martyr*. I've already done press once, but the studio is pushing it for the Oscars. So..."

"Is it that good?"

"It's based on a poem. 'Know ye the story of Queen Kelavane?'

The poem calls her that, but the movie calls her Ketevan. Hollywood and foreign names. But yeah, I think it's fairly good. We might have a shot at a couple of nominations."

Max said, "Wow. Good luck."

"Thanks. If we do get nominated, I'll have to go to the ceremony. I can get you a pass. You can come as security. Wear a suit."

"Fuck you in the bathroom."

Renee's ears burned, and she turned back to her computer to hide her smile. "These things can get crazy. Whatever happens, happens."

"I'll need a suit."

"Black suit, black tie, dark glasses," Renee said.

"Noted."

Renee was already excited at the prospect. She finished with her email and ventured out into the wider internet. It was early, but they could order in for dinner. She searched local restaurants to see if any of the delivery options were available. Wait times could be crazy even on the best of days, but being this close to Christmas would make it even worse.

"You said this Caravan movie was still in theaters?" Max said from the couch.

"Ketevan," Renee said. "Yeah, I'm pretty sure. Why?"

"We should go see it."

Renee laughed. "Yeah, sure."

Max sat up and put her feet on the floor. "Have you ever gone to see one of your movies?"

"Sure I've done it. At premieres or special events. I can't just walk into a theater that's showing one of my movies and sit there with my popcorn. People would notice. It would be a distraction. And then I would be the narcissist watching my own movie."

"So we'll go to a cheap theater, someplace where someone like you would *never* see a movie. So even if someone recognized you, they'd never believe it's actually you."

"Like seeing Elton John at Goodwill?"

Max grinned.

"Okay. But I also want to disguise myself at least a little."

"Do you really have anything in your closet that isn't designer?"

"I... am sure that I must."

Max shook her head and waved for Renee to follow her to the back door. "Come on. I've got to have something that will fit you.

I'll find an outfit, you look for showtimes."

There was a 5:15 showing of *Queen Martyr* at a North Hollywood theater and they had just enough time to change clothes and jump in the car. Renee wasn't entirely sure about her disguise: a pair of ripped jeans, a dark red hoodie, a black T-shirt so faded that she couldn't even make out the name of the band on the chest, and a baseball cap pulled low. She also took out her contacts and wore her glasses, hoping they would obscure the shape of her face enough to pass a cursory examination. That and the lack of makeup made her look different enough to keep anyone from looking twice.

They agreed Max would get the tickets and refreshments while Renee lingered at the back of the lobby and pretended to examine the movie posters. Renee was a touch uncomfortable, as she always was in public, worried that everyone who passed would recognize her. She was positive that a laugh from behind the counter was directed at her, or the kid lingering by the arcade games was actually trying to get a picture of her with his phone. She kept her head down, her fingers tucked into the pockets of her borrowed jeans, and tried to look casual. The clothes *were* ridiculously comfortable. Even the pockets were silky soft from repeated washes.

"Excuse me."

Renee tensed and turned toward the voice. A woman with a stroller gestured angrily at her.

"Would you mind not blocking the damn exit?"

"There are three other exits..."

The woman rolled her eyes and shoved ahead, forcing Renee to take a step back to avoid having her feet run over. "Unbelievable. God forbid you get inconvenienced. I'll just wait here until you deign to move."

Renee stared after the woman as she stormed out the door. Max arrived with two large sodas pinned against her chest with one arm, a bag of popcorn precariously held in the other hand.

"Everything okay?" Max asked.

"Yeah." Renee looked at Max's load and took the drinks from her. "It's... That woman was just incredibly rude to me."

"Some people are assholes."

"Not to celebrities, not usually." She looked at the people in the lobby with newfound appreciation. "I really am anonymous."

Max hooked her free hand on Renee's elbow and guided her toward their theater. "Yeah, and getting less so every second you stand here gawking. Come on, the previews are about to start."

Renee let herself be led. She watched the people behind the counter, not one of which even looked at her as she passed. She hadn't even realized how strangers would stare without staring, would tilt their heads, would be looking out the corner of their eyes when she passed their tables. Now she felt invisible in a way she didn't remember was possible.

She'd also forgotten what it was like to be in a theater where she wasn't a featured guest. The stadium seating was arranged so they entered the theater at the front of the audience, where everyone could potentially see her face. Fortunately the lights had already been turned down and the first trailer was booming loudly up on the screen, drawing all the eyes in the room. Only a handful of the seats were taken but Max marched up the stairs until they reached the very last row, against the back wall underneath three small windows where the projectionists could look out. Max let Renee take a seat in the corner, where she would have the least potential of being spied upon.

On the screen, a trailer was already playing An actor was running in an alley between two buildings. Renee leaned over to Max.

"That guy's an asshole. Half the people I know refuse to work with him."

"Huh," Max said. "Are you going to be doing that the whole time?"

Renee smirked. "No. I'll stop."

Max nodded and faced forward.

The first image of the movie was a close shot of Renee's face. It was covered with dirt, grime, and trails of blood ran down either side of her face. Her hair had been darkened and thin strands of it hung in her face. There was a fine sheen of sweat on her face and throat. She was staring at the ground gasping for breath until a shadow passed in front of her. She raised her eyes to face the person in front of her, curling her lip in disdain.

"One last entreaty?" Her voice was rough and weak, vaguely Russian-accented. "One last attempt to test my will?"

A metal spike was place between her eyebrows and moved slightly higher. Renee, Queen Ketevan, smiled and revealed she had blood on her teeth. The shot changed to show her persecutor, a dark-skinned man with a sharp chin and a narrow nose.

"Will you convert?"

"I shall rise to Heaven, where I will find your god and fuck him in the ass."

The man raised a hammer and swung it down. The screen smash-cut to black, but the impact was still heard loud enough to make several people in the audience jump and gasp. Max leaned over to Renee, who angled herself to hear the whispered comment.

"I somehow doubt those are her real last words."

"Historical accuracy is the first victim in stuff like this," Renee said back.

The black screen led into the title, and then opening credits. RENEE LAMAR was written large, in elegant red cursive. She was the only one who didn't have to share the screen with other names. After the first few names, the black faded to reveal a stone throne room. Renee was seated on a beautiful throne framed by a wooden structure that reminded her of a canopy bed. The scarlet cloth draped over it was the same color as her blood from the opening scene.

She looked vibrant and gorgeous, wearing all the finery one might expect from a queen. Her hair was completely covered by a complicated headdress, and she also wore a wimple that covered her neck. Max couldn't follow the dialogue, transfixed by every closeup of Renee. It was one thing to watch her on a large TV screen. It was quite another to see her face projected onto a wall. Her face had to span five feet from chin to forehead. Her eyes were in high definition, hyper-realistic, shining brighter than they did in real life.

Max moved her hand across the arm of the chair and slipped her fingers over Renee's thigh. Renee looked down but said nothing.

The first scene ended. Renee left the throne room and walked down a long corridor, two men trailing behind her. They were arguing about something, but they might as well have been speaking a foreign language for all Max cared. She wasn't even trying to comprehend the story anymore. She only cared about this massive Renee who suddenly filled up the world. The dark theater and everyone in it ceased to exist as Renee - Queen Ketevan - entered her private chambers. A maid appeared and helped her get out of the headdress. The men hovered by the door and continued their argument. It was something about kings and successions, about the queen's dead husband and which of her sons would assume the throne.

Max moved her hand to Renee's crotch. She pressed with all four fingers, and Renee shifted in the seat to push up against her. She picked up the popcorn bag and moved it so that anyone who happened to glance back wouldn't immediately notice where Max's hand was. Max appreciated the cover and took advantage of it immediately. She unzipped Renee's jeans and bit her bottom lip as she worked her hand into the fly.

Renee leaned toward her. "If you're going to do this, you have to make me come before the torture starts."

"How long do I have?" She could see in Renee's face that she was debating whether or not to tell the truth. If she said how long it really was, Max would draw out her orgasm for as long as possible. Max pressed her middle finger against Renee's underwear.

Renee stiffened and inhaled sharply. "About... about half an hour."

"Don't lie."

Renee glared at her. "Forty-five minutes."

"Okay."

Queen Ketevan ended the argument by snapping at the men, ordering them to send a message to someone or another, and then sent them out of her chambers. The maid continued taking off the queen's ornate costume until she was only in a pale brown shift. The queen sent her away as well. Once she was alone she took a deep breath and let her shoulders sagged. She walked to the window and looked out, her features twisted with internal conflict.

Renee shifted in her seat, her hand tight on the armrest. She choked back a grunt and pressed back hard against the seat.

"Are you naked in this one?"

"Not sexy," Renee said.

Max nodded. "Then I'll let you off easy."

"Let me off or get me off?"

Max chuckled, and then her fingers were inside Renee's underwear. Max leaned closer, her lips against Renee's ear.

"You look so fucking beautiful up there. I wish that maid would have undressed you completely. Taken you to a bath. Ran a cloth over your tits. Down between your legs. I wish I could have seen you ride her hand. I wish she would have whispered for you to come on her fingers. Come for me, Queen."

Renee closed her eyes and rolled her head back. "I can't believe I'm about to come in public... Oh god. Shit... shit, Max."

Max grinned and dropped her head to kiss Renee's neck as she came. When Renee relaxed, Max sank back into her own seat and looked back at the screen. Queen Ketevan was riding a horse on a beautiful green hill framed by snow-capped mountains behind her. The valley below had a lake so blue that she was almost positive it had to be computer generated.

"Where did you film this?"

Renee opened her eyes and stared ahead as if she'd just woken up and wasn't entirely sure where she was. "Georgia. We really went to Georgia for these shots. The one in, um, Asia."

Max raised an eyebrow and examined the screen again. The shot was absolutely gorgeous, and the music rose into a sweeping crescendo. Renee sat up straighter and put her hand on top of Max's.

"We should go."

"What? Why?"

Renee was looking at the screen, her expression wary. "I'm... I just know what's going to happen. I'm going to be locked up, starved, humiliated. And then I'm going to get beaten. Brutally. It's not going to be *Passion of the Christ*, but it's bad. I don't want you to see me like that. Not on a screen this big, and not with surround sound. And not with your fingers wet from getting me off. Please, Max."

"Okay," Max said. "We can go."

They stood up, leaving their popcorn behind in the seat. Max led the way down the stairs and turned to leave the theater, but she realized Renee had stopped at the bottom of the stadium seating and was looking back at the audience. Max walked back and stood behind Renee, her chin on Renee's shoulder and hands on her hips.

"Those are your people. Your fans. They're here to see you."

"Yeah," Renee said. Her voice was too soft for Max to read any emotion in it, either awe or terror, but she seemed strangely shrunken by the sight. She put her hand on top of Max's and laced their fingers together.

"Come on. Let's get out of here."

Max cast one more look at the screen, where a massive version of Renee stood tall and defiant as her hands and feet were shackled by heavy chains.

CHAPTER TWENTY-TWO

"THANKFULLY RETAINING *all of the charm that made its source material a runaway bestseller,* Never Lost Nobody *is at times triumphant, tragic, strange, and silly, but director LaSalle never lets it get too far away from the emotional heartbeat of the book. Renee Lamar anchors the film with the strength audiences have come to expect from her over the years.*"

Max broke the silence as she pulled into the garage. "There's something I want to show you."

Renee barely said a word during the drive, and she knew Max was worried about her. She wanted to say something to put her mind at ease, but she didn't know what to tell *herself*, let alone anyone else. She'd seen those people, all those anonymous strangers with their eyes locked on the screen, and she knew what they were about to see. Had they come out on this holiday to see a powerful woman making a stand? Or were they the sort of people who wanted the gore? The historical record was fairly detailed about how Ketevan was tortured, and their director had tried his best to be as accurate as possible. Seeing the dailies had turned her stomach, even though she knew it was all smoke and mirrors. Fake flesh, fake blood, but it was edited in such a way that it looked like spears glowing red-hot were being jabbed into her stomach.

She followed Max into the house. The sun had set while they

were in the movie. The staff at the theater had seen them leaving, and one girl asked if they wanted a refund. Max waved them off, claiming they had an emergency and it wasn't a problem with the movie. Renee had been grateful for the lie since she'd been unable to provide any explanation for herself. Now the house was dark, save for the kitchen light Max had turned on when she came inside. The living room was dark, which made the sunset view of the ocean out the window look like an illuminated painting.

Max sat at the kitchen counter with the laptop, typed a few words, and scrolled down a page. When she found what she was looking for, she got up off the stool and motioned for Renee to sit.

"Watch."

"What am I watching?"

Max pointed at the screen. It was a YouTube video paused on a brightly-lit blue square bordered by white ropes. A much-younger Max was standing in one corner.

"Is this your last fight? I don't want to see anyone die..."

"It's not that fight," Max said. "This was two years into my career."

Renee watched. Max's hair was shaved above the ears, leaving just a hint of black fuzz below a rooster's crest that hung limply across her forehead. She only had two tattoos, one on each shoulder. She wore blue gloves, a black jersey with grey accents, and white trunks. She danced in her corner, listened and nodded to someone on the outside of the ropes, and then faced into the ring. The other fighter had green gloves and a matching uniform. She had a cute face but her eyes were pure rage and anger. She rolled her shoulders back and forth, her lips puffed out around her mouth guard.

"Who..."

"Lucia Boldt," Max said. "I fucking hate those lime-green gloves."

The two fighters moved to the center of the ring where the referee urged them to 'keep it clean' and 'obey the rules at all times.' They touched gloves and retreated to their corners. Max seemed completely wired. She bounced on the balls of her feet. She held her arms out to either side and shook them like she was trying to dry off her hands. Boldt paced in a tight circle in her corner.

Renee put one hand against her mouth and chewed on her thumbnail. She remembered the shockwave that went through her when she saw Max go after Rand. That hadn't even been a fight, just a show of strength, and it made Renee wetter than she ever could have imagined. She wasn't used to seeing someone with so much power, or seen such power used so casually in a real-world situation. It was very clear that Max could have caused him grievous bodily harm. Knowing that made her softer touches mean even more. She didn't know how she would cope with seeing an actual fight.

A bell rang, and the two fighters converged. Max swung. Boldt easily avoided it. And from that moment on, the fight became something completely different.

Boldt recovered from her defensive swerve and came back with a blow to Max's head that sent her reeling. Max's hair flipped out of her face and her eyes went so wide that Renee could see the pupils were pointed in different directions. Dazed, swaying on her feet, Max threw a sloppy jab that had no hope of connecting. Boldt punched and Max stumbled back three steps. Boldt punched and Max brought both gloves up to protect her face. Boldt punched. Max crumpled.

The bell sounded again and Max finally hit her knees. The referee rushed to her, but Max waved him off and used the ropes to get back up. She hung on them as she made her way back to her corner. Her bottom lip was swollen and glistening with a spit-and-blood mix. More blood welled up from a cut above her right eye, which she was squeezing shut as she threw herself down on a stool and let her team take care of her.

"Why would you want me to see that?" Renee asked, twisting so she wouldn't have to see the screen anymore.

"This is the worst I was ever beaten," Max explained. "Amateur or pro. Lucia Boldt hurt me more than anybody before or since. At one point I honestly thought she'd split my skull in half. Look…"

She pointed at the screen. Max swung and connected with Boldt's jaw. Boldt barely registered the hit. Her uppercut seemed to come out of nowhere, scooping up from below and throwing Max's head back. Max tried to recover but tripped over her own feet. She hit the ground hard, both gloves up over her face even though Boldt was already backing off and the referee had knelt down beside her.

"Is that it?"

"Two more rounds," Max said. "The next day, the entire left side of my face was a bruise. It swelled to twice its size. I couldn't see out of that eye for… well, for a while."

Renee tapped a key to stop the video from playing out. She stood up and faced Max. "Why would you show me that?"

"You let yourself be vulnerable with me at the resort. I guess... to repay the favor. I don't like people seeing me like that. This fight was one of the most humiliating things that ever happened to me. I didn't think there was any way to recover from it. But six months later, in Las Vegas, I knocked out an odds-on favorite. I went from being a joke to being the underdog. And everyone loves an underdog."

"Yeah." She brought her hand up and let it hover for a moment, then touched Max's left cheek. "Here?" She leaned in and kissed the spot she had just seen swollen and bloody. Then she kissed higher, just above Max's eyebrow, where the cut had healed without leaving a scar. "I want to kiss every spot you've ever been broken. I want to make it better."

"That could take a while," Max warned her.

"I don't care." She licked her lips. "We didn't discuss the sleeping arrangements when we got back."

"I just assumed..." Max looked past Renee at the back door.

"That would be fine," Renee said, "but I would like it a lot better if you slept in my bed."

Max said, "For tonight?"

"For... as many nights as you'd like. And you. Not... Dr. Reszke or Mrs. Claus or anything like that. Just you. And just me, if that's acceptable to you."

Max nodded slowly. "If you're absolutely sure."

Instead of answering, Renee stepped closer and wrapped her arms around Max, one hand on her shoulder and the other in her hair as she leaned in for a kiss. Max pulled back before their lips could make contact.

"Same goes for you, then. No characters. No games. You have to be Renee Lamar. The real you, not some character, making love to a woman. Can you do that?"

Renee stared at her. She felt something unlock inside her, a door she'd long ago locked and sealed and sworn she would never reopen. But standing her with Max, all their insecurities out in the open, it felt wrong to keep it quiet.

"My name isn't Renee Lamar."

A wrinkle appeared between Max's eyebrows. "What?"

"I mean, it-it's my legal name. But it's not what I was born with. Until I was sixteen, my name was Renee Larcheveque. Dad was from Louisiana. I wanted to be an actress. I couldn't imagine people pronouncing that whole mess, so... I made it something prettier."

"Say it again?"

"Lar-chuh-vek."

"I don't think Lamar is prettier."

Renee smiled shyly. "Well. Not even Google knows about that name. So if it ends up in a tabloid, I know who to come after."

"Non-disclosure agreement, right?" Max said. "Besides, even without that, I have much better things to do with my mouth than blab your secrets."

"Name two."

Max smiled and kissed Renee.

Over the next half hour, she demonstrated at least three things she could do to keep her mouth occupied.

"Is it okay if I touch your scars?"

Renee's voice was barely a whisper, but it sounded echoing in the quiet of the bedroom. Max nodded and moved her head to see which one Renee would touch first. They were lying on top of the blankets, which had become tangled into a Gordian knot with the sheets during the course of the evening. Max was still naked, but Renee had gotten out of bed after their last round and retrieved a T-shirt from the hamper. Max had been running her fingers over it, admiring how soft the material was, when Renee asked her question.

"You can touch anything I have," Max said.

"Enticing offer." She rested her finger on a crescent arc on Max's ribs, just below her breast. "Not all of these can be from boxing."

"No," Max said. "I've lived a life."

Renee said, "A life where people hurt you."

Max said, "To be fair, sometimes I was trying to hurt them first." She kissed Renee's forehead.

"I can't imagine a life like that. I can't even remember the last time anyone made me bleed. I would probably faint."

They'd been lovers for over a week and, though Max hadn't been counting, but she estimated they'd had sex well over a dozen times. But somehow this felt more like a first time than many of her actual first times. There had been a connection, and a tenderness, that she usually didn't allow into her bed. This was supposed to be a perk of her new job. Banging the boss lady, going to bed with someone who literally had movie-star good looks. And now... she was lying here trying not to shiver as Renee's finger found another triangular mark.

"What did this?"

"Broken glass, bar fight. Guy got pissed off, slammed down my beer, glass shattered. I caught some shrapnel. In the gut. And here, on my hand."

"Where?"

"Here."

Renee lifted her head and tried to spot it in the dark. "I don't see it."

"I think only I can see it. Because I know where it is."

"Mm." Renee pulled Max to her and sank onto the pillow again. "We all have scars like that."

"Well, the interesting ones, anyway." Max moved her leg over Renee's hip and lifted herself, straddling her. Renee settled on her back and rested her hands on Max's hips. "Again?"

Renee parted her lips and looked down Max's body.

"You can ask for what you want," Max said. "I can always say no. But I can't read your mind. Tell me what you want, Renee."

"I want you to make me come again."

Max reached behind herself and stroked Renee's thigh. Renee parted her legs and moved her hands from Max's stomach to cover her mound.

"Your wish is my command, Ms. Larcheveque."

It was midnight when they finally realized they hadn't eaten all day, and Renee left Max in bed to go see what she could scrounge from the kitchen. She came back with two turkey sandwiches and a bag of chips, which they shared.

"It's been a long time since I made food for someone," Renee said.

Max peeled up one slice of bread and examined the interior. "You seem to remember the basics. Of course, it's pretty hard to screw up a sandwich."

"Once I figured out how long I should microwave the lettuce, it was smooth sailing." Max laughed, and Renee sat up straighter. "Wow. What was that?"

"A laugh. I laugh sometimes."

"That's very good to know."

They finished their sandwiches and then Renee went into the bathroom to brush her teeth. When she came back to tell Max she could borrow a brush, she found Max had fallen asleep curled around the bolster Renee usually kept at the bottom of the bed. Renee stared at her, this brute who had made a life letting people beat her up, this warrior who would take three punches before laying her opponent out with one, asleep in her bed.

It was like looking at a wild animal in a cage. She knew what those muscles could do when flexed. She'd seen those hands in action, and now the fingers were limply curled against the silky smooth slipcover of the pillow.

Renee tiptoed to the bed and laid down, careful not to disturb the mattress any more than necessary. She used her foot to pull the blanket up and untangled it, draping it across Max's naked body before she pulled it over her own. Max stirred.

"I should... go back to my room..."

"Sh," Renee whispered. "We're home. We agreed you'd sleep here tonight."

Max pushed herself up, laying her head on the pillow. "Oh... right..." She pushed the bolster away and held out her arm. "C'mere then."

Renee slid closer and let Max spoon against her side. She closed her eyes and debated what position she wanted. She could face Max, and they could embrace each other. Or she could turn away, and let Max press against her back like a shield against the world. Both options were very appealing in their own way.

She fell asleep trying to decide. She was also asleep before she realized that, for the first time in a very long while, she'd gotten into bed without even thinking about opening her teapot.

CHAPTER TWENTY-THREE

"EPIC, INSPIRING, *heartbreaking.* Queen Martyr *is the kind of film actors wait an entire career to find. This movie will be remembered for decades to come. If Renee Lamar never made another movie, her legacy in Hollywood is forever sealed with this tour-de-force historical drama.*"

The week between Christmas and New Year's was spent getting used to their new arrangement. Max wasn't entirely comfortable moving her things into the house, since their relationship was still technically new. Even if they were already living together, and even if Max was spending every night in Renee's bed rather than the one in the guest house, it seemed too soon to actually start nesting. So every night she prepared for bed in her own space, then went into the house to join Renee. Every morning, she went back out to shower and dress for the day.

Renee was also preparing for the *Queen Martyr* press junket. She would fly to New York, where she would appear on seven talk shows. Then to London for two more shows and a radio interview. Max's head spun whenever she looked at the itinerary. The jetlag alone was going to be a formidable enemy, but keeping on schedule with so many different shows, dealing with LAX, La Guardia, and Heathrow, was going to be hell.

"You don't have to come," Renee said in a tone that implied

she very much preferred having Max there. "Lillian agreed to pay your way, and I'm pretty sure everyone accepts the story that you're my private security. But it might be pressing our luck to travel together."

"No," Max said, "I want to be there for you."

"Are you sure?"

"I'm positive. It's all a bit overwhelming, but I'll get over it once the ball gets rolling."

Renee nodded and went back to packing, seemingly relieved by Max's answer. She was in the bedroom and Max was reading on the sofa when there was a knock on the door. She saw the time and stood up, already on her way to answer it.

"Renee, did you order lunch?"

"No, but that's a good idea," Renee called from the bedroom. "I'm starved."

Max looked through the peephole and was startled to see someone she recognized on the porch. "What the hell..." She opened the door and stared in confusion at Delia Hawkes. Delia's face broke into a beaming smile as soon as the door swung open. She was wearing a purple blazer and white slacks, and she had a manila envelope held in both hands like a process server.

"What are you doing here?" Max asked.

"I could ask you the same question. I thought you just happened to be sharing a wall with a celebrity at Halcyon. And now I find you answering the door at her house. That's more than a little curious, wouldn't you say? And what was the name you gave...? Dora Lincoln, wasn't it?"

Max was grateful she was fully dressed in jeans and a button-down shirt. Two days earlier, she'd been lounging in the living room in briefs and a tank top. There would have been no reasonable defense for that if she'd been caught, and she kicked herself for taking such a risk.

Delia continued speaking without waiting for an answer. "I'm here to have a business conversation with Ms. Lamar. Is she in?"

"I think if you want to talk with Ms. Lamar, you should call Lillian Swikert and make an appointment. Renee is very busy these next few weeks and she doesn't have time--"

"Oh, she'll make time for this." Delia's smile remained, but her eyes had become hard. "And I don't think she wants our conversation on anybody's calendar."

Renee had come out into the main room. "Max? Who is it?"

"Max," Delia repeated. "That name suits you much better, I have to say."

Renee joined them at the door. Max assumed she looked normal to the interloper, but she could see the tension in Renee's jaw. A few beads of sweat had appeared on her upper lip. There was a stranger standing on her porch. A stranger who knew who she was. Her privacy had been violated.

Someone had found her.

"You're the woman from Halcyon. The one who... I saw by the pool."

Delia's smile widened again. "That's correct. I'm so glad you remembered me. I was hoping that I would see Dora... excuse me, *Max*... again before I left, but after that first encounter she just seemed to vanish. I have to confess I was a little disappointed."

"How did you even find this address?"

Max looked at Renee, who was scanning the street behind Delia with increasing panic. It was clear she felt more exposed than usual, and the feeling was growing each second the door stayed open.

"Come inside," Max said.

Renee looked at her. Max nodded to her that it was okay, tacitly promising that she would handle anything that happened.

"Yes," Renee said, taking a step back into the relative security of the house. "Come inside. We can discuss this properly."

"Fantastic," Delia said, entering the house by stepping between them.

Max closed the door and caught Renee's eye.

Renee: *What is going on?*

Max: *I don't know. But I'll handle it.*

Delia had stopped at the edge of the living space. "Lovely home. Just spectacular."

"Thank you," Renee said warily. "What is this about?"

"Straight to business," Delia said. "I can respect that. This is about the new year, and your new career path. You and I are going to be working together a lot in the coming decade, Ms. Lamar, and I can't wait to get started."

Renee said, "I don't even know who you are or how you found my house. I'm very tempted to call the police."

"Oh, you don't want to do that," Delia said, completely unphased by the threat. "If you must know, Randall Hurley told me where you live. I reached out to him because I knew you two have been an item in the past. So I thought I would see if I could entice him to spill a few secrets. Turns out it was very easy. You must have done something to make him mad."

Max looked at Renee, who didn't take her eyes off Delia as she took out her phone. "I'm calling the police..."

Delia held up the manila envelope and tossed it onto the kitchen counter. "Look at that first. Then we'll talk."

Max retrieved the envelope. Inside were photos, poorly-lit but sharp enough to be certain of what they showed. It was Renee's room at Halcyon, apparently taken from outside through a gap in the curtains. Renee was on her back, propped up by a pillow with a clear shot of her face. Max was between her legs with her back to the camera and the strap of her harness visible around her waist. She was holding onto Renee's hips, caught in mid-thrust, and Renee's face was contorted in pleasure.

"What the fuck is this?" Max growled.

"I have to confess, I went to Halcyon hoping to make some connections. You could see how much luck I was having when you showed up. I guess it's the off season or something." She shrugged. "So one morning I snuck a peek into your room and got quite the eyeful."

The next photo showed Max on the edge of the bed with Renee kneeling between her legs, feet tucked under her ass and her head bowed, her purpose obvious from her posture. Max's hands were in Renee's hair. Even though her face was only visible in one photo, Max's tattoos made it clear she was the same person. And even without seeing Renee's face in the second picture, there could be little doubt of her identity. Renee had come to look over Max's shoulder, and she sucked in a breath.

"Oh, fuck..."

"If it would be cathartic to tear them up, feel free. I have plenty to spare. And they're on my phone, so..."

Max said, "Call the police, Renee."

Delia said, "I'll leave willingly. But just know that if I leave, I plan to post those on... well, wherever I can think of. I'm sure plenty of sites are willing to pay big bucks for uncensored pics of Renee Lamar's lesbian romp. The video will be the real moneymaker."

"Max, *stop*."

Max hadn't even realized she was moving until Renee's voice cut through the fugue. Delia did look concerned, and took a step back.

"What do you want?" Renee asked, her voice flat and cold.

"You..." Delia cleared her throat and forced herself to look away from Max. "You probably assume I want hush money. I don't. I want us both to make money. I want to work together. I'm a producer, but I'm looking to make my name as a director as well. I have scripts, I have a team, I just need people to give me a chance to make something truly special. Everyone out here has connections. They know people who know people who worked with people. I don't have that. I need an in. I need a Renee Lamar."

Renee said, "You're threatening me with this shit so I'll be in your... in some stupid straight-to-DVD movie?"

"For ten years," Delia said. "You're going to sign a contract to appear in any project I have over the next ten years."

"You're insane," Renee said.

"I'm focused and dedicated. People will see the movies because you're in them. You're going to set the ball rolling on my career. You'll be the Bruce Willis to my M. Night Shyamalan. We'll help each other. You get indie cred, people can see what I can do."

Max said, "You're a parasite."

Delia shrugged. "I use Renee's fame to get some of my own. And I guarantee that Renee always has work. No more dry spells, no more wondering if the offers will dry up because you'll always have work from me. And of course, if we're working together, I'll have no incentive to reveal your secret. We both benefit."

Renee said, "And if I say no, and you release those photos, no one in this town would ever work with you again. You'd be a pariah."

"Oh, please, I wouldn't take credit. And the places I sell them to will have a vested interest in keeping me anonymous. If I gave them a scoop like this once, maybe I'd be willing to do it again if the price is right."

Max had already mentally scripted three ways to get the woman out of the house. She looked at Renee. "I can make her leave."

It was said calmly, but she made sure Renee understood the implication of her offer. Renee shook her head. "Don't."

"Renee..."

"*Don't, Max.*"

Delia watched the exchange with a bemusement that indicated she was unaware of how much danger she was in.

"I'm not going to make a decision about the next ten years of my life while you're standing here with a knife to my throat. I need some time to think."

"Okay," Delia said. "But don't take too long. I already have a project you'd be perfect for and I want to get started on it as soon as possible. Let's say I'll have your answer by Monday morning. That will be a good time to hit social media." She walked to the door. "I'll see you around, ladies. Can't wait to work together."

She let herself out. Max crossed the living room in three steps and looked outside. She watched Delia go down the steps to an old red-brown sedan parked in front of the house. Renee, meanwhile, went into the kitchen and pulled a bottle from the cabinet. Max watched as she poured a glass, drained it, then poured a second that she could drink a little slower.

"I think I'm going to go for a drive."

Renee looked at her. "What? Right now?"

"Renee. I think... I'm going to go. For a drive."

They stared at each other across the kitchen counter. Renee seemed to know there was subtext to Max's comment, but she wasn't able to figure it out.

"And when I get back," Max said, "you won't have to make a decision."

Renee's eyes widened. "No."

"She's going to release those pictures eventually," Max said. "No one makes a threat like that without the intention to follow through. It doesn't matter how long you play her stupid game. Eventually you'll have a falling out and she'll pull the trigger anyway."

"I know." Renee looked into her glass. "And what happens? The world finds out I like women? I'm not going to ask you to hurt someone to keep that secret. And I'm... I'm not... I don't..." She closed her eyes. "Fuck her for making me feel like this is shameful. I-I-I hid it because it was private. Because it was nobody's business. But this bitch made it dirty. God, that pisses me off."

"So what do you plan to do about it?"

Renee chewed her bottom lip and stared at the wall. She drummed her fingers on the counter next to her glass, which was empty again.

"I need to make a phone call."

She left the kitchen and went toward her bedroom, but she stopped and looked back at Max.

"Would you have killed her?"

Max didn't hesitate. "I don't know. I would have hurt her. Bad. I don't know if I would have been able to stop myself. But I didn't care."

Renee's eyes drifted to the floor, then across to the window. She stared out at the ocean. Max remained where she was, waiting for approval or to be dismissed. Finally, Renee looked at her again.

"I'll never ask you to do that for me. I'd never want it. And knowing what happened to Miriam Rudd and how that affected you, the fact you would even bring it up... thank you."

"I wouldn't have offered for many people," she said.

"I know. That's what I'm thanking you for." She bit her bottom lip and left. Max let out a heavy breath and walked back to the window, making sure Delia was gone. When she read about Miriam's death, she'd sworn it would never happen again. She couldn't even get back into the ring without thinking about the darkness that descended over her mind. And while that same darkness had taken over her before, this time she could almost feel herself summoning it. She would have hurt Delia without regret. She would have killed her.

For Renee. To protect her, keep her safe.

Whatever that meant, and she was trying very hard not to dig too deep for meaning, she could no longer claim that protecting Renee Lamar was just a job.

CHAPTER TWENTY-FOUR

"WHILE DIRECTOR *Greg Brewster doesn't quite succeed at making Benedict Arnold a sympathetic figure in* To the Inhabitants of America, *he does manage to create a new villain in Arnold's wife, Peggy Shippen, a Lady Macbeth who manipulates her husband into turning against his country. Renee Lamar, always a fantastic addition to any movie, makes Shippen a well-rounded and believable villain. Lamar's career has always been lauded and now, with this brave and electric performance, the only thing we can be sure of is that Renee Lamar is only just getting started.*"

In the old days, not terribly long ago actually, Renee knew that this morning would involve going to a studio, speaking to a reporter, being surrounded by a camera crew and maybe a small audience, and having her interview aired on television. Now all she needed was a tablet with an internet connection. Lillian helped her set it up on a table in front of the living room windows so they could use the sun for natural light.

"Are you sure about doing it here?" Max asked. "The focus will be on you, but people will be able to see a lot of your house."

"It's okay," Renee said. "I need to feel comfortable, and I feel comfortable here. And I feel safe as long as you're with me."

Max squeezed her shoulder and stepped out of the way so the makeup girl could touch up something on Renee's cheek. Lillian was buzzing around the periphery, eyes locked on her cell phone.

"Okay, we're coming up on lunch, east coast time." She looked up and raised her eyebrows at Renee. "You ready, sweetheart?"

"As ready as I'll ever be."

Max gave her a thumbs up and moved out of the tablet's range. Renee leaned forward and held her finger over the button to start a live video. She closed her eyes, took a deep breath, and tapped the screen.

The button turned red.

Renee Lamar has started a live video.

Renee scooted back but remained hunched forward, arms in her lap with her fists pointing out. Her hair was tucked behind her ears to keep it from falling in her face. She smiled and held up one hand in a wave.

"Hello, all. I hope everyone's having an amazing week, and I hope everyone goes out to see *Queen Martyr* this weekend. We're really proud of it. I'm about to go on a press tour promoting the movie, so I wanted to spend a few minutes here talking about why the movie means so much to me. Queen Ketevan was a real queen who lived in the sixteen hundreds. She was a fierce but merciful queen. In the end, she was held prisoner by enemy forces who tried to make her convert to Islam. Ketevan refused even in the face of horrible torture.

"Ketevan stood by her ideals. She remained strong in her faith and refused to buckle even when it meant she could live. Her captors would have treated her as a queen if she accepted their faith, but she wouldn't do it. She couldn't do it. She refused to compromise. I felt empowered portraying this woman who went to her grave refusing to bow for something she didn't believe in. That resonated with me because I've been compromising for too long. I told myself it didn't matter, but suddenly it matters very much."

She rubbed her hands together and looked down at the floor. They'd planned this speech, her and Lillian, and she knew it perfectly. But this next part was hard to say out loud, especially knowing that so many people were already watching. She could look at the screen and see how many people were viewing it live, but she didn't dare. She looked up again and saw Max behind the tablet. Max met her gaze and nodded once, then winked. Renee smiled, grateful for the strength.

"I'm bisexual. My current partner happens to be a woman. Someone discovered this relationship, and invaded my privacy to take several lewd photographs. I was threatened with the release of this information, which made me realize that I refuse to treat my sexuality like something shameful. I blamed this person for making it dirty, but I was doing the same thing by keeping it a secret. So I don't want it to be a secret anymore.

"Hopefully this has taken away any incentive my blackmailer has to release those photographs. But if not, I hope they will be seen as what they are: a gross violation of my privacy. It doesn't matter who I was with in the pictures. It's nothing more than an invasion of my personal space, and I truly hope it is treated as such by anyone who is approached to purchase the images."

Her eye was drawn to the number of viewers, and she was startled to see it had risen into the thousands.

"I'm going to leave it at that right now. Um... in the next few weeks, I'm going to be making the rounds on talk shows to spread the word about *Queen Martyr*, and I'm sure this video is going to be brought up much more than I want it to. So hopefully if you have any questions, I'll answer them at that time. But if not, leave comments. I'll do my best to read and respond to them. I want to thank you for your support over the years, and for being there for every premiere and every film, from blockbusters to the biggest bombs. I'm not hiding anymore.

"Thank you, I love you, and I hope to see you all very soon."

She kissed her fingers and swept the kiss toward the screen, then tapped the button again.

This live video has ended.

"Perfect," Lillian said. "That was absolutely perfect. How do you feel?"

Renee slumped back in her seat. "Exhausted. Was it really okay?"

"It was great," Max said.

"So what happens now?" Renee asked.

Lillian said, "Now we go on as planned. Like you said, this is probably going to come up during interviews for *Queen Martyr*. We should be prepared for that."

"I want them to ask," Renee said.

"Okay. Then we prep like always. We keep an eye out on the

tabloids and the porn sites to see if anything shows up, but I don't think this Delia person has much wiggle room. If anything gets posted anywhere, our legal department has a lawsuit ready to go. And it goes without question that the bitch has burned every potential bridge she might have had in this town. She's completely finished."

"Do you think there's a market for what she's selling?" Max asked.

Lillian rolled her eyes. "There's always a market for smut. Especially of celebrities. I'm sure it'll get leaked out to some site or another. But we know what to look for, so we can put a kibosh on it pretty easily. In the meantime, you don't have to worry. Just keep doing your job and let us worry about doing ours. Everything will work out in the end."

Renee said, "So what now?"

"Now," Lillian said, picking up the tablet and flipping the cover closed, "you stay off the internet for the rest of the day. I have no doubt you're already getting comments from all sides of the spectrum. Reading them isn't going to do anyone any good. So my people and I will monitor that and keep you apprised of everything you need to know. And um..." She looked around for Max, who had somehow vanished in the past few seconds. "Um, you can take the time to decide how open you want to be about your relationship."

"I hope you're not telling me to dump Max."

"Not at all. You can tell everyone about her or you can ask that her privacy be respected. But you have to decide early because once you choose a route, you can't go back and unring the bell. Metaphors got mixed. But you understand what I'm saying?"

Renee nodded. "I do."

"Then okay. Call if you need anything. You were great today. Love you."

"You too."

When Lillian was gone, Renee stood up and went to find Max. It wasn't a long search; a quick glance outside revealed she was sitting on the edge of the pool with her feet in the water. Renee stepped out of her shoes and went to join her. Max was holding the bottle of water she'd been nursing all morning, pinching the label with one hand while turning the bottle with the other, slowly peeling it off.

"Mind if I join you?"

"It's your pool."

Renee pulled up her pants legs and sat down. The water was freezing, and she hissed between her teeth as she got used to the temperature. Max finished peeling the label and put it on the stone beside her.

"What's on your mind?" Renee finally asked.

"Big step in there."

"Mm-hmm."

"Told the whole world your partner was a woman."

Renee nodded. "Yep."

"'Partner'."

"Oh." Renee pushed one foot through the water and watched the ripples. "We haven't really talked about labels. But we've been sleeping together for a couple of weeks now. I don't want to stop any time soon. Unless..."

"No, I don't want to stop."

"Okay, then. Well. Partner seemed more accurate than girlfriend."

Max grunted. "I do hate that word."

"It's very high school."

"Yeah. Partner's fine. I don't mind partner."

Renee nodded.

"It won't be an issue? Someone like you dating someone..."

"Someone...?" Renee prompted.

"A tattooed has-been who, until a few months ago, had a double-digit bank account balance."

Renee smiled. "The alternative being, what, someone like me? An actress with the same insane schedule and matching neuroses? That sounds incredibly boring. Not to mention narcissistic. I want a beautiful woman who is like no one I've ever seen before. I want a woman who has artwork that only I get to see on a regular basis. Someone who barely speaks but, when she does speak, she makes sure every person in the room pays attention. But more than that, I want someone I can trust. Someone who makes me feel safe and protected."

Max moved her feet under the water. "Okay."

"If anything, I'm worried you'll get bored with me. I'm not sure what I have to offer besides a pretty face and a lot of money."

Max looked at her. "You think I would have offered to kill someone for a pretty face? And I don't care about money. In fact, if we're going to be partners, you should probably stop paying me."

"You'll still be my security," Renee said. "You should be paid for the job you're doing."

"Okay, but we should make some kind of... arrangement about it. Have that Lillian woman hire me through the studio. Make it an actual job and not just a wad of cash you deposit in my account every month."

"We can do that."

Max nodded and faced forward. "A pretty face. God. Do you really think that's all you have to offer me?"

"Enlighten me, please."

Max sighed, clearly annoyed she would have to spell it out. She tilted her head back and looked at the sky. Renee swept her foot back and forth as she waited.

"Home. Peace. Stillness." She exhaled and slumped her shoulders. "I've been falling since the fight with Miriam Rudd. Just that... stumbling and helpless kind of falling where you never actually hit the floor. Then you came into my life and you gave me a purpose. You gave me something to care about. Someone to worry about. You woke me up."

Renee smiled and ducked her head. "Wow."

"Yeah. This... I mean... what we're doing... I understand if you don't want to stake your coming out on it. It's good. We're happy. But it doesn't have to be forever. You don't have to decide right now if we're... if *I'm* going to be... you know..."

"My happily ever after."

"Right."

Renee nodded. "I know. We're not there yet. But I'm happy where things are right now."

"Me too."

"On that subject," Renee said, "being happy. The... the pills. I know you don't like them."

Max shook her head. "It's not my place, as your partner or security."

"Be that as it may, I haven't been needing them as much lately. But I have been craving them. I want to take them all the time. I hate that feeling, but I hate giving into it even more. I want to stop. I've been trying to stop. I always eventually give in, and that's another feeling I hate. I only started taking the damn things to feel good, and now they're the main reason I feel like shit. I can't go straight into rehab because of the press tour. And it would look terrible if I came out of the closet and went right to a treatment center. So I need your help. I need you to help me get clean."

"It's not going to be easy."

"I know. And I know you're not a professional. It's not ideal. But I trust you. I probably trust you more than anyone at this point. It's a big ask, I know..."

"I'll help you."

Renee looked at her. "Are you sure?"

"Mm-hmm. You should probably keep them around for the press tour. Just to maintain, you know, everything. You don't want to be going through withdrawal and jetlag while everyone with a talk show is asking about your biggest secret. But once we're home, in your safe space, I'll help you."

Renee put her hand down on the stone lip of the pool. After a moment, Max put her hand on top of it. Their fingers laced together with very little effort.

"Thank you."

"Of course."

Renee smiled. She understood what that meant, in this context and from this person. Max would never have said 'you're welcome.' She said 'of course' because in her mind, there was no question. There was no doubt. Renee needed help. Of course Max would do everything in her power to provide it. They'd found each other at the exact right moment. Renee, just barely keeping her head above water, flailing around for anything that might pull her back to shore. Max, adrift and lost who apparently hadn't even noticed how far from land she'd drifted.

And somehow, in the midst of drowning, they'd found each other. They clung to one another, fought the undertow, and pulled each other back to solid ground.

She didn't know how long her relationship with Max would last. It was extremely possible they could have a falling out while on tour. Those things were notorious for destroying relationships. Max might hate how long Renee had to be gone for filming. Renee might realize she didn't like sharing her space with Max. There were an infinite number of wrong paths they could take, pitfalls they could stumble into. Basically, they had saved each other from drowning, but they were still a long way from shore.

Renee let go of Max's hand, leaning to one side so she could reach into her pocket. She took out her phone and billfold, gently tossing them back away from the pool's edge.

Max watched her. "What are you doing?"

"Come on."

Renee smiled and pushed herself forward, sinking into the pool. They were still close to the shallow end, but the water still reached just above Renee's belt. She smiled and held out her hand to Max, who was staring at her incredulously.

"You're crazy."

"I used to worry about that, actually," Renee said. "But now, who cares. Maybe I am crazy. It'll make life more interesting." She backed away from Max with her hand still out as she moved into the deeper end. "Come on. I need you to keep my head above water."

Max sighed a laugh and shook her head, then began emptying her own pockets. Renee, confident she'd won the standoff, moved further into the pool and bent her knees. She took in a deep breath of air just before she went under, arms spreading out to either side as she sank. There was a displacement in the water, a current that washed over her, and then powerful arms wrapped around her torso. She was pulled up, gasping when she hit air again. Her hair covered her face like a thick red sheet, and she swept it out of the way just before her lips were captured in a kiss.

She clung to Max, wrapping both legs around her underwater. Max planted her feet on the bottom of the pool, the water so deep that the waves they were making splashed against the sides and back of her head. Renee felt it pooling between their bodies, going down Max's shirt and between the buttons of hers, but she didn't care. She had a feeling Max didn't care, either. The future didn't matter. If they stayed together, if they broke up, it was a moot point because she'd been forever changed by the woman currently holding her. She knew Max had been changed as well. She could hear it in how easily she spoke, the way she no longer stopped herself from speaking too much.

Renee broke the kiss and looked into Max's eyes. Max's hair was too short to obscure her vision, but Renee pushed it back anyway and turned it into a crown of unruly spikes. She laughed at the sight, and Max smiled in response.

"How do you feel?" Max asked.

It was a simple question but the answer was huge. She was out of the closet. She was going to get off the pills. She had cut toxic people out of her life. She was being held in the arms of a woman she might very soon admit she had fallen in love with, a woman she believed loved her back. She had protected her career from potential ruin, which had only served as a realization of just how much potential she had. She could make movies she truly cared about, movies that meant something, movies that could change lives. All she had to do was ask and the scripts would come. It seemed impossible to condense that all down into a single answer. Except no... it wasn't impossible at all.

"Free," she said. "I feel free."

Max smiled, and Renee cupped the back of her head to pull her close so they could resume the kiss. When their lips met, Max bent her knees and they went underwater again. Renee tightened her grip on Max but she didn't stop the kiss and she didn't panic. She knew the surface was right above them, and she knew Max would take them back up before she needed another breath.

But for now, in this moment, she was going to enjoy the sinking.

ABOUT THE AUTHOR

Geonn Cannon is the author of over fifty novels, including the Riley Parra series which was adapted into an Emmy-nominated webseries by Tello Films. He's also written two tie-in novels for the television series Stargate SG-1. He was the first male author to win a Golden Crown Literary Society Award for his novel Gemini, and he won a second for Dogs of War. Information about his other works and an archive of free stories can be found online at geonncannon.com.